Acclaim for Jennifer Egan's

EMERALD CITY

"Accomplished. . . . She brings us to the transcendent place where reality becomes illusion." - *—Newsday*

"Egan is a skillful writer with a good eye, a smooth yet passionate style." *—San Francisco Chronicle*

"Egan's voice is boundless. . . . The moment of change is so carefully constructed in each story, so fascinating in Ms. Egan's offhand way, that one recognizes a great new writer." *—The Dallas Morning News*

"Immediately apparent is Egan's versatility, and the confidence she has to create such dramatically different characters from numerous backgrounds." *—Bookends*

"Distant settings and enticing writing . . . all bear the unmistakable stamp of a rising talent at work. . . . Egan takes chances, ventures afar." *—Seattle Post-Intelligencer*

"Egan displays a mastery of voice for a young writer. . . . Her voice moves easily and accurately between characters, her stories as beautifully crafted as they are darkly moving." *—Charlotte Observer*

"Both *Emerald City* and *The Invisible Circus* shimmer with moments when everyday life seems imbued with intimations of the marvelous. . . . Egan's finely polished gems, mined from the expanse of her rich imagination, will surely retain their literary luster." *—NewCity's Literary Supplement*

JENNIFER EGAN

EMERALD CITY

Jennifer Egan is the author of *A Visit from the Goon Squad* (which won the Pulitzer Prize, the National Book Critics Circle Award, and was a finalist for the PEN/Faulkner Award); *The Keep*; *Look at Me* (a National Book Award finalist); *The Invisible Circus;* and the story collection *Emerald City*. Her stories have been published in *The New Yorker, Harper's Magazine, GQ, Zoetrope, All-Story,* and *Ploughshares,* and her nonfiction appears frequently in *The New York Times Magazine.* Egan lives with her husband and sons in Brooklyn.

www.jenniferegan.com

Jennifer Egan is available for lectures and readings. For information regarding her availability, please visit www.rhspeakers.com or call 212-572-2013.

EMERALD
CITY

EMERALD CITY

JENNIFER EGAN

Stories

ANCHOR BOOKS
A Division of Random House, Inc.
New York

FIRST ANCHOR BOOKS EDITION, OCTOBER 2007

The stories in this collection have appeared, in slightly different form, in the following publications: "Why China?" "The Stylist," and "Sisters of the Moon" in *The New Yorker*; "Sacred Heart" in *New England Review* and *Best of New England Review*; "Emerald City" in *Mademoiselle* (as "Another Pretty Face") and *Voices of the Xiled*; "The Watch Trick" and "Passing the Hat" in *GQ*; "Puerto Vallarta" in *Ploughshares* and *Prize Stories 1993: The O. Henry Awards*; "Spanish Winter" in *Ploughshares*; "One Piece" in *The North American Review*; "Letter to Josephine" in *Boulevard*.

The Library of Congress has cataloged the Nan A. Talese / Doubleday edition as follows:
Egan, Jennifer.
Emerald city : stories / Jennifer Egan. —1st ed. in the U.S.A.
p. cm.
1. Manners and customs—Fiction. I. Title.
PS3555.G292E44 1996
813'.54—dc20
95-35956

Anchor ISBN: 978-0-307-38753-0

www.anchorbooks.com

Printed in the United States of America
10 9 8 7 6 5 4 3

For David Herskovits

For their guidance and support during the years I spent writing these stories, I am grateful to the following: Tom Jenks, Daniel Menaker, Mary Beth Hughes, Ruth Danon, Romulus Linney, Philip Schultz, Diana Cavallo, Daniel Hoffman, Don Lee, Virginia Barber, Jennifer Rudolph Walsh, Nan A. Talese, Jesse Cohen, Diane Marcus, the National Endowment for the Arts, the New York Foundation for the Arts, and the Corporation of Yaddo.

CONTENTS

Why China?   1

Sacred Heart   27

Emerald City   41

The Stylist   57

One Piece   72

The Watch Trick   89

Passing the Hat   105

Puerto Vallarta   116

Spanish Winter   133

Letter to Josephine   147

Sisters of the Moon   167

WHY CHINA?

It was him, no question. The same guy. I spotted him from far away, some angle of his head or chin that made my stomach jump before I even realized who I was looking at. I made my way toward him around the acupuncturists, the herbal doctors slapping mustard-colored poultices on bloody wounds, and the vendors of the platform shoes and polyester bell-bottoms everyone in Kunming was mysteriously wearing. I was afraid he'd recognize me. Then it hit me that I'd still been beardless when he'd ripped me off, two years before, and my beard—according to old friends, who were uniformly staggered by the sight of me—had completely transformed (for the better, I kept waiting to hear) my appearance.

We were the only two Westerners at this outdoor market, which was a long bike ride from my hotel and seedy in a way I couldn't pin down. The guy saw me coming. "Howdy," he said.

"Hello," I replied. It was definitely him. I always notice eyes, and his were a funny gray-green—bright, with long lashes like little kids have. He'd been wearing a suit when I met him, and a short ponytail, which at that particular moment signified hip Wall Street. One look and you saw the life: Jeep Wrangler, brand-new skis, fledgling art collection that, if he'd had balls enough to venture beyond Fischl and Schnabel and Basquiat, might have included a piece by my wife. He'd been the sort of New Yorker we San Franciscans are slightly in awe of. Now his hair was short, unevenly cut, and he wore some kind of woven jacket.

"You been here long?" I asked.

"Here where?"

"China."

"Eight months," he said. "I work for the *China Times*."

I stuffed my hands in my pockets, feeling weirdly self-conscious, like I was the one with something to hide. "You working on something now?"

"Drugs," he said.

"I thought there weren't any over here."

He leaned toward me, half smiling. "You're standing in the heroin capital of China."

"No shit," I said.

He rolled on the balls of his feet. I knew it was time to bid polite farewell and move on, but I stayed where I was.

"You with a tour?" he finally asked.

"Just my wife and kids. We're trying to get a train to Chengdu, been waiting five days."

"What's the problem?"

"*Mei you,*" I said, quoting the ubiquitous Chinese term for

2

"can't be done." But you never know what, or which factors, if changed, would make that "no" a "yes." "That's what the hotel people keep saying."

"Fuck the hotel," he said.

We stood a moment in silence, then he checked his watch. "Look, if you want to hang out a couple of minutes, I can probably get you those tickets," he said.

He wandered off and said a few words to a lame Chinese albino crouched near a building alongside the market. *China Times,* I thought. Like hell. Heroin pusher was more like it. At the same time, there was an undeniable thrill in being near this guy. He was a crook—I knew it, but he had no idea I knew. I enjoyed having this over him; it almost made up for the twenty-five grand he'd conned out of me.

We set off on our bicycles back toward the center of town. With Caroline and the girls I took taxis, which could mean anything from an automobile to a cart pulled by some thin, sweating guy on a bicycle. It pissed me off that the four of us couldn't ride bikes together like any other Chinese family. ("Since when are we a Chinese family, Sam?" was my wife's reply.) But the girls pleaded terror of falling off the bikes and getting crushed by the thick, clattering columns of riders, all ringing their tinny, useless bells. Secretly, I believed that what really turned my daughters off were the crummy black bikes the Chinese rode—such a far cry from the shiny five- and ten-speeds Melissa and Kylie had been reared on.

In our previous encounter, his name had been Cameron Pierce. Now, as we rode, he introduced himself as Stuart Peale, shouting over the thunderous racket of passing trucks. The names fit him exactly, both times; Cameron had had the impatient, visionary air of a guy who thinks he can make you a shitload of money; Stuart was soft-spoken, a sharp observer—what you'd expect from a reporter. I told him my name—Sam Lafferty—half hoping he'd make the connection, but only when I named the company I traded for did I notice him pause for a second.

"I've taken a leave while they investigate me," I said, to my own astonishment.

"Investigate you for what?"

"Messing with the numbers." And unnerved though I was by what I'd revealed, I felt a mad urge to continue. "It's just internal at this point."

"Wow," he said, giving me an odd look. "Good luck."

We dismounted in front of a large concrete kiosk teeming with several lines of people all shoving and elbowing one another good-naturedly toward a ticket counter in a manner I'd decided was uniquely Chinese. Stuart spoke to a uniformed official in vehement but (I sensed) broken Chinese, gesturing at me. At last the official led us grudgingly through a side door and down a dimly lit corridor that had the smudged, institutional feel of the public schools I'd attended as a kid and made sure my daughters would never go near.

"Where is it you're headed—Chengdu?" he called.

We had entered a shabby office where a military-looking woman sat behind a desk, seeming thoroughly disgruntled at Stuart's intrusion. "Yes—for four people," I reminded him.

Within minutes, I'd handed Stuart a wad of cash and he'd given me the tickets. We reemerged into the tepid, dusty sunlight. "You leave tomorrow," he said. "Eight-thirty A.M. They'd only sell me first class—hope that's okay."

"It's fine." We always rode first class. So had Stuart, I guessed, in his prior incarnation. "Thank you," I said. "Jesus."

He waved it away. "They don't want Americans having a lousy time over here," he said. "You point out that it's happening, they'll fix it."

He handed me his card, the address in English and Chinese, the *China Times* logo neatly embossed. Still a pro, I thought.

"You live in Xi'an," I remarked. "We may go there, check out that clay army."

"Look me up," he said, clearly not meaning it.

"Thanks again."

"Forget it," he said, then mounted his bicycle and rode away.

"A total stranger?" my wife said, back in our hotel room, where I'd surprised her with the train tickets. "He just did this, for no reason?"

"He was American." I was dying to tell her he was the cocksucker who'd conned me, but how could I explain having hung out with the guy, having accepted a favor from him? I knew how Caroline would see it: one more incident in the string of odd things I'd been doing since the investigation began, the most recent of which was to beg my family to drop everything and come with me to China. It wasn't depression, exactly; more a weird, restless pressure that made me wander the house late at night, opening the best bottles of wine in our cellar and drinking them alone while I channel-surfed along the forgotten byways of cable TV.

"Where are the girls?" I said. "I got them each a little knife to peel pears with."

"You bought them knives?"

"Just little ones," I said. "Have you noticed how the old ladies are always peeling pears? I've got a feeling there's something on those skins they shouldn't be eating."

Caroline had washed her bras and underpants and was hanging them on the open dresser drawers to dry. In the late seventies, before we married, we'd spent a year in Kenya with the Peace Corps. Caroline washed her clothes the same way over there, hanging them on strings she tied across our tiny room. I used to watch her through the web of strings and underclothes—her reddish brown hair and deep, peaceful eyes that made me think of amber. I always liked remembering that time, knowing the money and houses and trips we'd gotten our hands on since hadn't washed it all away. We're still those people, I'd tell myself, who helped the Masai to repair their houses made of cow dung.

Caroline opened a window, and instantly the sour, bodily smell of China poured into the room. "A perfect stranger," she mused, smiling at me. "Must've been that sweet face of yours."

My daughters give me away. They are blond, expensive-looking creatures whose soft skin and upturned noses I used to take credit—wrongly, I know—for having procured for them at great cost, as I had their orthodontically perfect smiles. In Kenya the Masai children had dry lips and flies in their eyes. Memories of their deprivation had overwhelmed me in recent months, for reasons unknown. I'd find myself staring at my daughters accusingly, awaiting some acknowledgment from them of the brutal disparity between the Masai kids' lives and their own. Instead, I found in their beauty a righteousness that galled me. The Avenging Angels, I'd started calling them, which perplexed my wife.

Not that my daughters were identical. They were ten and twelve years old, the younger one deeply in awe of the elder, Melissa, whose figure-skating prowess had lent her a kind of celebrity at their private grammar school. Melissa was also, the world seemed to agree, fractionally more lovely. Determined to correct this imbalance, I had lately become the fervid champion of Kylie, my youngest, a campaign my wife deplored and begged me to abandon. "Picking favorites is awful, Sam," she told me. "Melissa thinks you hate her."

"The world picked. I'm just evening up the balance."

But there was something heavy-handed in the sudden barrage of affection I lavished on Kylie. She rose to the occasion, gamely enduring our "special" trips to the zoo and the Exploratorium and Ocean Beach, where we stumped through the damp, heavy sand, both wishing (or I was, at least) that Melissa—whom I'd bluntly excluded, whose skating competitions I often pretended to doze through—were with us.

But now their hatred of China, their deep resentment at having to spend the best part of their summer in a land where people blew their noses without Kleenex, had united Melissa and Kylie in steely mutiny against me. "Daddy, why?" had been their refrain from the moment the trip began: the boat from Hong Kong into Canton, the days of waiting for a plane to Kunming that, when it finally arrived, could not have inspired less confidence had we assembled it ourselves. "Why, Daddy?" With time the object of their query had grown more and more diffuse: Why here? Why any of this? They were asking the wrong man.

The buildings of Chengdu were newer, and therefore less pleasing, than those of Kunming. I roamed the streets impatiently, my wife and listless daughters in tow. We drank green tea in a moist enclave beside a Buddhist temple. The fog smelled of chemicals. An Asian girl with strange pale-blue eyes kept staring at us. "Do you think she might be crazy, Dad?" Melissa asked.

"She's admiring your haircut."

Melissa glanced at me, thinking I might be serious, then recognized the acid sarcasm that had become my preferred mode of speech with her of late.

"Probably had you for a dad," she muttered.

"Probably wasn't so lucky."

My wife sighed. "She's blind," she said. And instantly I saw that

Caroline was right; the girl was drawn by our unrecognizable voices, but her eyes were empty.

"Let's go to Xi'an," I said. "It's supposed to be fascinating."

Melissa opened our guidebook, scanned the pages, and read aloud: "The Qin Terra-Cotta Warriors are one of the few reasons to visit Xi'an, an urban wasteland of uniform city blocks and Soviet-style apartment buildings, but they are a compelling one."

"That's not what I heard," I said, suppressing an urge to knock the book out of her hands.

"Terra-cotta worriers?" Kylie said.

"Heard from who?" my wife asked.

"The guy who got us the train tickets."

"They're thousands of clay soldiers as big as real men," Caroline explained to Kylie. "A paranoid Chinese emperor had them built underground to protect him after he died."

"Neat," Kylie said.

Caroline looked at me. "Let's go there."

"Why?" Melissa asked, but no one answered.

Looking downtrodden, Melissa wandered out first from the tea shop. As we followed her, I turned to glance behind me, and sure enough, the Asian girl with the pale-blue eyes was still gazing blindly after us.

I knew—and Caroline knew—that since the investigation began, my status had slipped—or risen—from that of her husband and equal to that of a person she indulged. Gratitude and guilt played a part in this. I'd worked my ass off at the office for years while she puttered away in her sculpture studio. Then, three years ago, Caroline hit the jackpot, landing a piece in the Whitney Biennial. This led to more exhibits, one-person shows in several cities, including New York, and dozens of studio visits from thin, beautiful women and their sleek young husbands who smelled (like me, I suppose) of fresh cash, or from scrawny, perfumed old bats whose doddering mates brought to mind country houses and slobbering retrievers. Everything my wife had yet to sculpt for the next three years was already sold. We'd talked about my quitting, pursuing anthropology or social work like I'd always said I wanted to, or just relaxing, for Christ's sake. But our overhead was so high: the house in Presidio Terrace, the girls in private school heading toward college, skating lessons, riding lessons, piano lessons, tennis camp in the summers— I wanted them to have all of it, all of it and more, for the rest of their lives. Even Caroline's respectable income could not have begun to sustain it. Then let's change, she'd said. Let's scale back. But the idea filled me with dread; I wasn't a sculptor, I wasn't a painter, I wasn't a person who made things. What I'd busted my chops all these years to create was precisely the life we led now. If we tossed that away, what would have been the point?

We were still chewing on this when I found out about the investigation. Its architect, the aptly named Jeffrey Fox, had been after my scalp for years because his wife, Sheila, was a ball-buster, whereas mine was lovely and terrific. He was always sniffing around Caroline's studio, and had bought three of her pieces the year before. "That little turd!" Caroline had shrieked when I told her about the investigation, and night after night we'd sat awake long after the girls were in bed, holding whispered conferences on how I should respond: Write a letter to the board proclaiming my innocence? Mount a counteroffensive against Fox? But no, we decided. The best thing to do, for the moment, was nothing. Let the investigation run its course, and when it turned up nada, question the legitimacy of its having been started at all. In the meantime, take a leave, clear my head, get some sleep. Ha-ha.

The unlikely, intangible result of all this was that Caroline owed me. I knew it, she knew it, and I won't lie—this was not a feeling I minded.

My wife and daughters stared morosely from the taxi windows as we sped from the Xi'an airport to the Golden Flower hotel, past block after block of drab apartment buildings and sidewalks lined with limp, dusty trees. The opulent hotel boosted everyone's spirits; nothing like the sight of uniformed doormen, marble floors, and rich Midwesterners patting their billfolds to renew one's faith in the bounty of the universe. To my secret delight, not even Caroline cared to accompany me into "old" Xi'an, which, according to the Asian woman in a collegiate headband behind the front desk (no doubt she was the product of classes in how to look and act Western), was where I would find Stuart's address. I left Caroline sprawled on the bed boning up on Qin Shi Huangdi, the maniac emperor who'd built the terra-cotta warriors—at the cost of many a laborer, she reported; the final masterpiece contained not only the blood and sweat of its sculptors, but occasionally even their flesh.

On the streets of "old" Xi'an I found the lady tea vendors out in force—women whose idea of washing a glass was to sprinkle water on it. I hadn't let my daughters near these people, convinced that their unwashed glasses harbored all manner of deadly diseases just waiting for the chance to invade my girls' frail intestines. But I bought myself a glass of tea and sipped it, bought one of those fluffy white buns filled with a suspicious mash of vegetables and scarfed it down, then bought a second. I felt terrific.

I wandered inside a Buddhist temple and heard people chanting to this delicate sound of chimes, and my stomach was fluttery in a way I remembered from childhood, the feeling you had shoplifting, or creeping into the next-door neighbor's basement. I left the temple, savoring this as I walked to Stuart's street, when suddenly, from half a block away, I saw him. He was standing right there on the sidewalk, talking with three old Chinese ladies. My heart leapt— there is no other way to put it. The blood rushed to my face the way it used to when I'd just seen a girl I wanted to put the moves on, and then I stopped dead. What in hell was the matter with me? This was a man, after all—a man who'd ripped me off and made me look like an ass. Was I losing my mind? But already I'd started walking again, toward him.

"Stuart," I said. He looked blank, and I felt weirdly crushed. "Kunming, remember?" I said. "You got us the tickets."

"Oh. Right." He gave a baffled smile. The Chinese ladies moved away.

"We made it," I said, idiotically.

There was an awkward silence. "So, you still writing about drugs?" I asked.

"This week it's smuggling."

"Smuggling what?"

"Antiques. People leaving the country with vases and stuff."

"You sort of specialize in crime stories?" I asked, my pulse firing like a machine gun.

"It's an area I know pretty well."

"From experience." I couldn't stop myself.

Stuart cocked his head. "You sort of a would-be journalist?"

"Either that or a would-be criminal," I said, and burst out laughing.

Stuart said nothing. He took a long look at me, and I saw in his face the first sign of real curiosity.

"Anything to see around here besides those clay warriors?" I asked.

"Not much in Xi'an," he said. "Tomorrow I'm going to some Buddhist caves outside town that are pretty extraordinary."

"Is that right?"

"You're welcome, if you can sneak away," he said. "But you'd have to stay overnight."

"Might be doable."

He named a place at the train station and said he would wait there at ten the next morning. "If you can make it, great," he said, turning to go.

"I'll be there," I said.

Brady bonds, emerging markets: these were much on Cameron Pierce's mind at Harry Meyer's stag party, where I met him the first time. Olive-green suit, ponytail, an air of having more cowboy in him than the rest of us. How did Harry know him? Harry was tables away, a wet shirt draped over his head, trashed. It wasn't long before the strippers showed up, three of them, each with different-colored hair, and while they went to work on Harry, Cameron told me about the limited partnerships he was setting up to invest in African countries: Nigeria, Ivory Coast, Botswana, Zimbabwe.

"You spend much time over there?" I asked.

He'd pulled a red apple from the centerpiece and was eating it with a fierce pleasure that made me want one, too. "As much as possible," he said, grinning.

"I hear you," I said. And, on impulse, I told him about my stint with the Peace Corps—something I rarely mentioned to people in the business.

Cameron set down his apple core and leaned toward me so that I could hear him over the hoots and catcalls issuing from our colleagues. "That's what makes all this bullshit worthwhile," he said. "Getting out. Seeing what's really there." We understood each other then; we were separate from—better than—what surrounded us.

The next week, Cameron Pierce's lackey made a presentation at

our office. One of our junior traders, Burt Phelps, seemed as interested in the deal as I was but wanted to do more checks on Pierce,
or at least wait until Harry Meyer came back from his honeymoon
on Bora Bora so we could run it by him. "Feel free," I said. "I'm
going in." I was operating on pure gut, that great, impulsive organ
we traders live by. And because he felt like an asshole, I guess, Burt
went in, too. Both of us put up the minimum—twenty-five thou-
sand. The lackey came to pick up our certified checks.

Cameron and I talked on the phone a couple of times after that.
He was heading for the Far East. "That's the place," he said. "You
want to get lost, do it there." We agreed to have lunch after he got
back. My monthly statements started coming in; with returns at
twenty percent, I couldn't complain. Burt was over the moon. Then
I guess we sort of forgot about it. I'd got four statements in all when
they stopped arriving, but it was two months at least before I noticed, and then only when Burt mentioned it. "Sam, you heard
anything lately from Africo?" he said.

The rest was straight out of bad TV: calls to the Africo office
hitting a disconnected line; a trip to the Kearny Street address on
Cameron Pierce's business card revealing that Africo, Ltd., had
never been there. Nor was it registered with the SEC or anywhere
else; ditto for Cameron Pierce and his lackey, whose name I can't
remember now. Harry Meyer, whom we'd forgotten even to consult,
had never heard of the guy. "Cameron who? My party?" he said,
perplexed. "Someone else must have brought him." In other words,
they were con men. We'd been had. Not that unusual in a business
like ours, where guys had so much cash to throw around. But the
ones it happened to were usually younger, more junior than me.
More like Burt. And it was Burt who'd had the reservations.

In the world of lousy investments, twenty-five grand isn't much
to lose. But I couldn't get over it. The guy had sat there selling me

on his phony deal, and while I was thinking how much I liked him, how good it all sounded, he was thinking, He's nibbling, no question. Peace Corps?—oh shit, I've got him now! The guys at work teased me about the fine example I'd set; Caroline wrung her hands a little over the money; then they all pretty much forgot about it. But not me. I kept thinking of him, Cameron Pierce, wondering how many "partners" he'd brought in, how many "deals" he'd pulled off in the past. He was somewhere—lying on a beach, smoking cigars, spending our money. At night, while Caroline slept, I'd find myself wondering who he was, really, at the very bottom. Was he anyone?

If I'd really listened to the guy, I decided, I would've seen it coming. Hadn't he practically told me? I'm from another world, he'd said—a place where this one means nothing. I'd assured him that I was, too. But it wasn't true. I'd played by the rules. And he'd won.

"What kind of bullshit is this?" Caroline said when I'd outlined for her what struck me as a perfectly reasonable plan: while she and the girls visited the Qin terra-cotta warriors the following day, I would take an overnight trip with a total stranger to another part of China.

"The same guy who got us the tickets?" she said. "He lives in Xi'an? Why didn't you tell me that before?"

"I wasn't sure how you'd react."

"Why should I care?"

"You seem to care now."

"Now that I know you kept it a secret, I care. Now that you've decided to disappear with him, yes, Sam, I care."

We stared at each other, furious. "Is this sexual?" Caroline asked in disbelief.

"Oh, Christ in holy heaven!" I thundered.

My wife studied me. After a long while she said, "We're not doing this, Sam."

"Not doing what?"

"Whatever it is you're trying to do."

"I'm going with him."

"Fine," she said. "We'll come, too."

We stood mournfully in the long, snaking line of Chinese peasants waiting to board the train. Melissa and Kylie were doing their best to sulk, but their utter mystification at our sudden change of plans and the appearance of a stranger in our midst interfered with the purity of their displeasure. I went with Stuart to buy the tickets—his, too; it seemed the least I could do after he'd so gracefully agreed to bring my entire family with him to the Buddhist caves. He took off to do an errand before the train left.

"Is this a train to the worriers, Daddy?" Kylie asked.

"The warriors are for tourists," I said.

"But wasn't that the whole point of coming here?" Melissa asked. "For the terra-cotta warriors?"

"You're welcome to stay and see them," I said. "Personally, the obsessions of some whacked-out king are about the last thing I'm in the mood for."

"Why don't we wait in the first class lounge so the girls can sit down?" my wife suggested.

"We're riding hard-seat," I said. "It's only eight hours."

The girls looked aghast. I watched them cast baleful looks their mother's way, and saw, in their silky, seamless faces, the thick patina so many years of privilege had left behind. Suddenly I was enraged —enraged at both of them for not knowing what these privileges had cost.

"You can wait in line with the rest of the world," I said. "It won't kill you."

Crestfallen, they gazed at me—their father, who rarely let them ride a bus for fear of all the germs and scrofulous characters they might encounter.

"Your father's afraid that if we ride first class, his friend will be disappointed in us," Caroline said acidly.

"He's not my friend," I said.

"Then whose friend is he?" she asked.

For every square inch of hard-seat, there were roughly twenty-five people anxious to sit down, bringing to mind the phrase "lousy food and not enough of it." The majority of passengers were peasant boys, barefoot, their rolled-up pants exposing those dark round scars they all seemed to have from the knee down. They'd been shopping in Xi'an and now were loaded up with identical cheap zippered bags half bursting with booty. There were no seats for my daughters, and I watched their faces fill with fear at finding themselves caught in the press of sweating, seething humanity I'd taught them to avoid. To my relief, several peasant boys leapt from their seats to make room for the girls, who ended up next to a window, facing each other. Caroline sat near them, still angry, avoiding my eyes. Stuart stood off to one side, already looking weary of us.

The hours drifted past. I kept an eye on my daughters, watching their sullenness give way to a kind of solemnity, acknowledgment of a situation that was obviously bigger than they were. Each time the train eased to a stop at a platform, food vendors swarmed around outside its windows, pushing tiny carts. After the first two hours, Kylie and Melissa were in there with the best of them, dangling fistfuls of limp bills to buy homemade popsicles on toothpicks, plastic bags full of tiny green apples, and squares of coarse yellow cake. Everything they bought, they offered to their neighbors. This broke my heart.

The land got very strange. Gray hills bulged from the earth in such a way that their middles looked wider than their bases. "It's like Dr. Seuss," I overheard Kylie say. Caroline sketched in her notebook. I stared out the window at the weird hills and told myself that we lived in San Francisco, in a house on Washington Street that I'd bought for a million in cash six years ago, that our house existed right now, the burglar alarm on, automatic sprinklers set to keep the garden alive. It's all still there, I thought. Waiting. But I didn't believe it.

We reached our destination late that afternoon—the sun still high but pouring out thick, stale light. Our presence seemed more of a novelty here than it had anywhere else we'd been, and as we tottered toward the street, passersby gathered around to stare at us in unabashed amazement.

The *binguan,* or tourist hotel, could easily have doubled as a jail: small rooms each containing two narrow, squeaking beds; dirty concrete floors; communal "bathrooms"—a row of holes in the concrete—no paper, no doors, big flies drunk on the stench from below. "My God," I told Caroline, frantic when I saw the arrangements, "there's no way we can stay here."

"I should think you'd be delighted."

"There's got to be a better hotel in this town!"

"This is a tiny little town, Sam. Why should there be another hotel?"

"Shit." I was starting to sweat. "What're we going to do?"

"Relax," Caroline said. "It's one night."

"But the girls. Jesus!"

"We're okay, Daddy," piped Kylie from the next room.

I rushed over there to find her hunched on her cot, looking out the grimy window at a long outdoor trough lined with faucets—our sink—where Melissa was washing her face. I sat on Kylie's bed and put my arm around her. "I love you, baby," I said. "You know that." She nodded and slumped against me. Melissa returned to the room, dripping water and shivering.

"It's cold," she said.

"Get a towel," I told her.

"There aren't any."

I looked around. "How can there not be towels?"

"There's no hot water either, Dad," Melissa said. "Or soap." She threw herself on her cot to a yelp from the rusty springs and stared at the ceiling.

I watched helplessly as her long hair gathered on the grimy floor. Then I felt Kylie shaking beside me and peered at her wet, streaked face. "Oh, baby, stop," I said. "Please, what's wrong? Tell Daddy."

"I'm scared," Kylie said through chattering teeth.

"Scared of what? What's scaring you?"

Melissa sighed from her bed.

"What if we never go home?" Kylie asked in a small, strained voice.

"Of course we'll go home," I said. "This is just a vacation."

For a long time no one spoke. I held on to Kylie and stared challengingly at Melissa, my oldest, waiting for her to snort or wince —to betray her scorn in the smallest way. But Melissa lay still, her eyes closed, arms crossed on her chest.

What exactly Stuart made of the bedraggled and downcast group he led to dinner, God only knew. I sensed that we amused him. The city felt like a place the world had forgotten: dusty streets, a department store whose listless, utilitarian window displays reminded me of South Dakota, where I grew up—those yellow sheets of plastic they hung inside store windows to keep out the glare. I remembered kicking stones as I peered through that yellow plastic at outdated transistor radios that I didn't dare even ask my luckless father to buy me, and promising myself I'd have enough money someday to buy the whole fucking store, if I wanted.

At a restaurant bizarrely named Wine Bar, we dined on bowls of scalding broth mixed with soy sauce and two raw eggs, which instantly boiled. The other diners ceased eating and gathered around to more fully enjoy the spectacle of our presence. Soon a modest crowd pushed in from the street through the open door or pressed faces to windows, peering in at us.

Stuart turned to the girls. "How much do you hate China?" he asked.

They glanced nervously at me. "Just a little," Kylie said.

"More than anything." Melissa, of course.

"What's the worst thing about it?" Stuart asked.

After some consideration, they agreed that the raucous throat-clearing and spitting on the pavement were the worst.

"In India, they spit red," Stuart said.

"Gross," said Melissa. "Why?"

"They chew a red nut, and it makes them spit. So they spit red."

"Do you hate it here, too?" Melissa asked in a sweet, bantering voice I almost never heard her use anymore.

"Me, I love it," he said. "You know every minute how far away you are."

"Isn't that true anywhere in the Third World?" Caroline said. "India, say, or Africa?"

"Too much suffering," Stuart said. "Unless you're there to help the people, what's the point? But in China, everyone eats."

"Our dad did that," Melissa said. "He went to Africa and he fed the kids."

There was a respectful pause. "Peace Corps?" Stuart asked.

"We went together," Caroline said, taking a sip from my bowl.

Outside, the night fell dingy and red. Trailed by a small crowd of spectators, we walked to a market where vendors displayed piles of black grapes on thin cloths spread over the pavement. We hadn't seen grapes in China before, and Melissa and Kylie each bought a bunch. The grapes were hard and sweet. Stuart bought some fresh walnuts, which he carried over to us in his untucked plaid shirt. The girls each took one. "But how do we break it?" Kylie asked.

"Ah, that's the best part," Stuart said. He placed a nut on the pavement and split it with the heel of his boot. It made a satisfying crack. The meat inside was a glistening white. We all got into it, cracking walnut shells with our shoes, pulling the sweet white meat from inside while a crowd of our Chinese hosts eyed us with bemused perplexity. "Americans," I imagined them saying, afterward. "The poor sons of bitches have everything in the world, but they've never tasted fresh walnuts."

As we walked back toward our *binguan* in the quiet dark, Melissa stopped, turned suddenly to all of us, and announced, "This was the most fun day in China."

Night in that town was heavy and black as the ocean. Caroline and I lay on our separate cots, both wide awake. "I'm having a disturbing thought," she said. "A feeling, really."

"I'll lie with you," I said, finding the floor with my feet.

"Wait," she said. "Let me say it."

I lay back down. There was a long silence, during which I

discovered that I was afraid—physically afraid—for the first time in as long as I could remember.

"You did it," Caroline said. "Isn't that right?"

"Did what?" But I knew.

"Took the money. Or whatever it was."

"Jeffrey Fox has been whispering in your ear."

She ignored me. "I started thinking it a couple of days ago," she said. "I don't even know why. Tell me," she said, and I heard her turning to face me. "I won't blame you."

"Yes," I said.

"Sam. Why?"

"I don't know." It was the truth.

"Did you feel pressure? Financial pressure?"

"Maybe. I don't know."

I listened for some sound, some relief from any direction, but there was nothing. We were alone in the middle of nowhere. Of course, I thought—I'd dragged them to a place where they couldn't help but see it.

"Remember that prick who ripped me off?" I said. "That friend of Harry's who turned out not to be?"

"Yes . . ."

"He was— That was— It started then."

I heard a rustle of coarse sheets, and Caroline was beside me—her warm, familiar skin, the soft shirt she slept in when we traveled. "Sam, I'm so sorry," she said. She held me, her strong warm arms around my neck, and suddenly I was sorry, too, to see, for the first time, what I had become.

It looked like the dead of night when Stuart roused us. Loudspeakers filled the streets, blaring some awful, tinny wake-up music accompanied by saccharine female singing. The street lights were a stark, fluorescent white. We sat on an empty bus, sat and sat, waiting for it to fill. As the first light streaked the sky, we finally started to move.

Caroline and I were in opposite seats, Kylie beside me, Melissa next to her. Stuart sat directly in front of me. By now he felt like family, somehow—enough to eliminate the need for talk at this hour. At last the bus swung out of town. The sun came up. Peasants got on, some carrying chickens, one clutching a pig. Most were folded into sleep the instant they sat down. My girls slept. After a while Stuart slept, too, his head back against the window, mouth open slightly. I got a long, close look at his face in profile, studied his pores and Adam's apple, and found myself wondering who the hell he was. He looked like anyone. I tried to remember Cameron Pierce at Harry's party, but the vision of him that had haunted me these past two years was gone. So then, how did I know this guy was the one? I tried to put myself back in Kunming, where I'd recognized him. Eyes? Chin? But that encounter, too, was murky now. Stuart was a guy sleeping inches away, his expression not much different from my daughters'. And then I was terrified: of having put my family in the hands of a total stranger—not the man who had robbed me.

By the time we hit the wooded hills, the sun was up. The land looked unkempt, trees pushing and shoving against each other like people fighting their way through lines in China. Stuart woke and glanced at me, then turned to the window. "Almost there," he said.

We got off near a cluster of flimsy kiosks that marked the beginning of a path into the hills. The kiosks apparently doubled as overnight shelter for their proprietors, who were just beginning to stir. I heard more wake-up music from somewhere, but a powerful wind gushed through the trees and drowned out most of it. I was filled with a sense that something was about to happen. As Stuart led the way uphill, I took Caroline's hand. I saw Kylie reach for Stuart's hand—she's confused, I thought; she thinks he's me. But Stuart took her hand, and they walked together so naturally that I was sure he had a daughter, and a wife, too. He must have all this, somewhere. My legs burned as we climbed.

At the top of the hill, we came upon the base of a towering wall of sheer cliff, red-tinted like clay, pocked with rows of small openings that had to be the caves. A scaffolding of sorts had been erected for scaling this vertical surface, and we mounted a set of stairs and began to climb, Stuart first, still holding Kylie's hand, then Caroline and me. Melissa came last, looking tired and unsteady. I decided then to end my campaign against her.

We got off the stairs at the very top. There, beyond a series of curved openings in the rock, were the caves, their walls stained with bright, extraordinary colors, massive painted wooden Buddhas and Buddha-like attendants towering within each. "My Lord," Caroline said. Kylie and Melissa just stared.

My wife and daughters went ahead. I let them go, stopping before three caves that had been linked to accommodate one massive Buddha lying horizontally. He was half sleeping, it seemed, his almond-shaped eyes just slightly open, his head wider than the length of me. For a long time I stared at the Buddha. Then I turned to lean over the railing and look back down the mountainside.

Stuart joined me. "Well, here it is," he said. "As promised."

"You outdid yourself."

"So. What happens now?"

"Good question," I said, and laughed. "Now I go to jail."

There was a startled pause, then Stuart laughed, too. "Hell," he said, "don't do that."

"They've got me."

"I don't think you'll go to jail," he said.

He was probably right—the publicity would be too damaging. Something quiet and equitable was more like it: pay up, then fuck off. But our lifestyle would suffer, no question.

"Anyway," Stuart said, looking down the mountain, "I don't see any SEC here."

"The world isn't that big."

"It's big enough."

The sounds of Caroline and the girls were just scraps, tossed up by the wind, then washed away. I leaned over the railing, feeling the calm weight of the Buddha behind me. "You ripped me off," I said. "Twenty-five grand. In San Francisco." I was afraid, almost whispering. But I wanted him to know the world wasn't as big as he thought.

"Wasn't it fifty?" he said.

I stared at him, a part of me thinking, Of course. "You knew? All this time, you knew?"

"Pretty much. Once or twice I started thinking I might be nuts."

"I don't believe this," I said. "Why didn't you run?"

"From what?"

"But I mean—why help me? Why bring us all the way here?"

"Bring you!" he said, and laughed. "You begged to come. Fucking chased me to Xi'an."

I said nothing. What a horse's ass I'd been.

"Why?" Stuart asked, and in the silence I felt the prickle of his curiosity. He moved closer. "Why follow me? What did you want?"

"I was afraid you'd get away."

Stuart laughed, perplexed. "I am away."

And of course this was true, he'd got away two years ago. And ever since, I'd been filled with disgust at the waste of my life.

"It's my daughters," I said. "They've done me in. Drained me dry."

"They're good kids," Stuart said quietly.

I listened for them, as I'm always half listening for my family. But I couldn't hear them anymore, not a wisp of their voices or laughter.

"How does it feel, doing what you do?" I asked.

Stuart laughed. "Like everything feels when it's you," he said. "Like nothing."

I turned to him. He looked small—one small man, alone in the middle of China. And I thought I saw in him some diminishment or regret—as if Stuart's fortunes, too, had slipped since our previous meeting. I thought, He has nothing but his freedom.

"Where are they?" I asked, anxious for my family.

"Gone," he said. "You drove them away."

I grinned, uneasy. "Fuck you."

"Fuck you, too."

"I believe you did."

The wind blew away our laughter.

Stuart walked us back to the bus. Then, to our surprise, he said he wasn't going with us.

"Why?" cried the girls, with such keen disappointment that I felt a flicker of jealousy.

"Going to hang out here a little," he said. "Do some communing with the Buddhas."

"Do you ever get to San Francisco?" Caroline asked.

Stuart grinned at me. "Now and then."

Kylie clapped her hands. "Come to our house!"

"I might just do that," Stuart said, and I saw, to my relief, that he wasn't serious.

"Please," Melissa said. "You can watch me skate."

"All right, all right. Let's get on the bus," I said.

Stuart waited outside, then waved goodbye as we pulled away. Melissa sat alone. I moved next to her and put my arm around her small, athletic shoulders. But the gesture felt awkward. And I was struck by how long it had been—months and months—since I'd shown the slightest affection toward my oldest daughter. She seemed hardly to notice, twisting to look out the window at Stuart, whose narrow back we could barely see making its way uphill. When finally she turned back around, I stared at her, amazed that a twelve-year-old girl could hold so much sadness in her face. "He was nice," Melissa said.

SACRED HEART

In ninth grade I was a great admirer of Jesus Christ. He was everywhere at Sacred Heart: perched over doorways and in corners, peering from calendars and felt wall hangings. I liked his woeful eyebrows and the way his thin, delicate legs crossed at the ankles. The stained-glass windows in our chapel looked like piles of wet candy to me, and from the organ came sounds that seemed to rise from another world, a world of ecstasy and violence. I longed to go there, wherever it was, and when they told us to pray for our families, I secretly prayed for the chance.

We had a new girl in class that year whose name was Amanda. She had short red hair and wore thin synthetic kneesocks tinted different colors from the wash. She wore silver bracelets embedded with chunks of turquoise, and would cross her legs and stare into space in a way that suggested she lived a dark and troubled life. We were the same, I thought, though Amanda didn't know it.

During Mass I once saw her scrape something onto a pew with the sharp end of a pin she was wearing. Later, when the chapel was empty, I sneaked back to see what it was and found her single first initial: A. To leave one's mark on a church pew seemed a wondrous and terrible thing, and I found myself watching Amanda more often after that. I tried talking to her once, but she twirled her pen against her cheek and fixed her gaze somewhere to my left. Close up, her eyes looked cracked and oddly lifeless, like mosaics I'd seen pictures of in our religion class.

Though we were only girls at Sacred Heart, there were boys to contend with. They came from St. Pete's, our companion school three blocks away, and skulked relentlessly at the entrances and exits of our building. Unlike Christ, who was gentle and sad, these boys were prone to fits of hysterical laughter without cause. I was unnerved by stories I had heard of them tampering with the holy wafers and taking swigs of the sacred wines Father Damian kept in his cabinet. They reminded me of those big dogs that leap from nowhere and bark convulsively, stranding children near fences. I kept my distance from these boys, and when the girls began to vie for their attention, I avoided them, too.

Late in the fall of that ninth-grade year, I saw Amanda cutting her arm in the girls' room. I pretended not to notice, but when I left the stall and began washing my hands, she was still there, her wrist laid out on the wood box that covered the radiator. She was jamming a bobby pin into the skin of her forearm, bunching it up.

"What are you doing?" I asked.

Amanda glanced at me without expression, and I moved a step closer. She was working her arm in the fierce, quiet way you might work a splinter from your foot.

"It's not sharp enough," she said impatiently, indicating the bobby pin. It was straightened into a line, and the plastic nubs at its ends were gone. Amanda seemed unembarrassed by my presence, as though cutting her arm were no weirder than braiding her hair with ribbons. This intrigued me, and her urgency drew me in.

I was wearing a pin, a white goat my mother's husband, Julius, had bought me on a trip to Switzerland. I wore it to please my mother, for though a nicer man than Julius was hard to imagine, I just couldn't like him. It was as if my not liking him had been decided beforehand by someone else, and I were following orders. Now, as I touched this present from him, I wanted Amanda to use it —I craved it like you crave a certain taste. It was wrong and bad and exactly right. I felt a pleasant twisting in my stomach, and my hands shook as I unhooked the pin from my dress.

"Here," I said, holding it up. "Try this."

Amanda's face turned softer than normal. She held me with her eyes while I looked for a match to sterilize the pin. A lot of furtive smoking went on in that bathroom, and I found a book wedged behind the mirror. I took off my goat's head pin and held its sharp point in the flame until it turned black. I tried to give the pin to Amanda, but she shook her head.

"You," she said.

I stood there a moment, holding the goat. Although I was frightened, there was something raw and beautiful in the sight of Amanda's smooth white arm against the chipped paint of the radiator cover. Gently I took her wrist and touched the pin to the scratch she had already made. Then I pulled it away. "I can't," I said.

Her face went slack. When I tried again to give her the pin, she turned away from me, embarrassed. I felt like a coward, and knew for sure that unless I helped Amanda to cut herself, she would never be my friend.

"Wait," I said.

I took her wrist and held it. I scraped the pin hard this time and made a thin, bleeding scratch. I kept going, not afraid anymore, and was surprised to find that the sharp point made a sound against her skin, as though I were scraping a piece of thick fabric. It was hard work, and soon my arms were shaking. Sweat gathered on my forehead. I did not look once at Amanda until I had finished an A like the one she'd carved on the pew. When finally I did look, I found her eyes squeezed shut, her lips drawn back as if she were smiling.

"It's finished," I told her, and let go.

When Amanda opened her eyes, tears ran from them, and she rubbed them away with her other hand. I found that I was crying, too, partly with relief at having finished, partly from some sorrow I didn't understand. In silence we watched her arm, which looked small and feverish under its bright tattoo. I noticed the hot light overhead, smells of chalk and disinfectant, my own pounding heart. Finally Amanda smoothed her hair and pulled her sweater sleeve down. She smiled at me—a thin smile—and kissed me on the lips. For an instant I felt her weight against me, the solidity of her, then she was gone.

Alone in the bathroom, I noticed her blood on my fingers. It was reddish orange, sticky and thin like the residue of some sweet. A wave of despair made me shut my eyes and lean against the sink. Slowly I washed my hands and my goat pin, which I stuck in my pocket. Then I stood for a while and stared at the radiator, trying to remember each thing, the order of it all. But already it had faded.

From that day on, when I looked at Amanda a warm feeling rose from my stomach to my throat. When I walked into class, the first place I looked was her desk, and if she was talking to somebody else, I felt almost sick. I knew each detail of Amanda: her soiled-looking hands with their bitten nails, the deep and fragile cleft at the base of her neck. Her skin was dry and white around the kneecaps, and this got worse as fall wore on. I adored these imperfections—each weakness made Amanda seem more tender, more desperate for my help. I was haunted by the thought that I had seen her blood, and would search her distracted eyes for some evidence of that encounter, some hint of our closeness. But her look was always vague, as if I were a girl she had met once, a long time ago, and couldn't quite place.

At that time I lived in a tall apartment building with my mother and Julius, her husband of several months. Julius was a furrier. The previous Christmas he had given me a short fox-fur coat that still draped a padded hanger in my closet. I hadn't worn it. Now that it was almost winter, I worried that my mother would make me put it on, saying Julius's feelings would be hurt. His lips seemed unnaturally wet, as though he'd forgotten to swallow for too long. He urged me to call him "Dad," which I avoided by referring to him always as "you" and looking directly at him when I spoke. I would search our apartment until I found him, rather than have to call out. Once, when I was phoning my mother from school, Julius answered. I said "Hello . . ." and then panicked over what to call him. I hung up and prayed he hadn't recognized my voice. He never mentioned it.

It was getting near Christmas. Along the wind-beaten streets of downtown the windows were filled with cotton-bearded Santas and sleighs heaped high with gifts. It grew darker inside the Sacred Heart chapel, and candles on thin gold saucers made halos of light on its stone walls. During Mass I would close my eyes and imagine the infant Christ on his bale of straw, the barn animals with burrs and bits of hay caught in their soft fur. I would gaze at our thin Jesus perched above the altar and think of what violence he had suffered since his day of birth, what pity he deserved. And I found, to my confusion, that I was jealous of him.

Amanda grew thinner as winter wore on. Her long kneesocks slipped and pooled in folds around her ankles. Her face was drawn to a point and sometimes feverish, so her eyes looked glossy as white marbles against its flush. Our homeroom teacher, Sister Wolf, let her wear a turquoise sweater studded with yellow spots after Amanda explained that neither one of her parents was home and she had shrunk her uniform sweater by accident. That same day her nose began to bleed in science class, and I watched Sister Donovan stand for fifteen minutes behind her desk, cupping Amanda's head in her palm while another girl caught the dark flow of her blood in a towel. Amanda's eyes were closed, the lids faintly moist. As I stared at her frail hands, the blue chill marbling the skin of her calves, I knew that nothing mattered more to me than she did. My mouth filled with a salty taste I couldn't swallow, and my head began to ache. I would do anything for her. So much love felt dangerous, and even amid the familiar, dull surroundings of my classroom, I was afraid.

Later that day, I saw Amanda resting outside on a bench. With my heart knocking in my chest, I forced myself to sit beside her. I glanced at her arm, but her sweater sleeves reached the tops of her wrists.

"Are your parents on vacation?" I asked.

"They're getting a divorce."

Uttered by Amanda, the word sounded splendid to me, a chain of bright railway cars sliding over well-oiled tracks. Divorce.

"My parents are divorced," I told her, but it hissed when I said it, like something being stepped on.

Amanda looked at me directly for the first time since that day in the girls' room, weeks before. Her irises were broken glass. "They are?" she asked.

"My father lives in California."

I longed to recount my entire life to Amanda, beginning with the Devil's Paint Pots I had visited with my father at Disneyland when I was six. These were craters filled with thick, bubbling liquids, each a different color. They gave off steam. My father and I had ridden past them on the backs of donkeys. I hadn't seen him since.

"I have a brother," Amanda said.

The Devil's Paint Pots bubbled lavishly in my mind, but I said nothing about them. Amanda crossed her legs and rapidly moved one foot. She fiddled with her bracelets.

"Why do you watch me all the time?" she asked.

A hot blush flooded my face and neck. "I don't know."

Our silence filled with the shouts of younger children swinging on the rings and bars. I thought of the days when I, too, used to hang upside down from those bars, their cold metal stinging the backs of my knees. I hadn't cared if my dress flopped past my head and flaunted my underwear. But it was ninth grade now, and nothing was the same.

"If you could have one wish," Amanda said, looking at me sideways with her broken eyes, "what would it be?"

I thought about it. There were plenty of things I wanted: to poke freely through the cupboards of our altar, to eat communion wafers by the fistful and take a gulp of the sacred wine. But I told Amanda, "I'd wish to be you."

I had never seen her really smile before. Her teeth were slightly discolored, and her gums seemed redder than most people's. "You're crazy," she said, shaking her head. "You're really nuts."

She hunched over and made a high, thin sound like a damp cloth wiping a mirror. I thought at first that her nose was bleeding again, but when I leaned over to look at her face, I saw she was only laughing.

————

Each morning, as the arc of frost on my windowpane grew taller, I worried about the coat. It hung in my closet like an eager pet I knew I would have to feed eventually. When I touched the soft fur, it swung a little. I had an urge sometimes to stroke it.

While I was dressing for school one day, my mother came into my room. Her face was puffy with sleep, her lips very pale. It still amazed me to think that she and Julius shared the big bed where she had slept alone so many years, where I had slept, too, when I had nightmares. I imagined an extra room where Julius slept, an inner door outside which he and my mother kissed good night and then did not meet again until morning.

"It's cold outside," my mother said.

I nodded, scanning my closet for a sweater. I could feel her watching the coat. She was quiet while I pulled on my kneesocks.

"You know," she said, "Julius really likes you. He thinks you're terrific." Her voice was filled with pleasure, as if just saying his name felt good.

"I know it," I said. And I did—he fixed me pancakes in the morning and had offered many times to take me to his warehouse, where I pictured row after row of soft, beckoning furs. "Pretty soon," I would mutter vaguely.

"Sarah," my mother said, and waited for me to look at her. "Please won't you wear it?"

She had flat hair and an open, pleading face. When she was dressed up and wearing her makeup, my mother could look beautiful to me. But now, in the early white light of a winter morning as she balanced her cup on her kneecap, she looked worn out and sad.

"I will," I said, meaning it now. "I'll wear the coat when it's freezing."

―――――――

Two weeks before the start of Christmas vacation, Amanda wasn't in school. When I saw her empty chair, I felt a flicker of dread. I came inside the classroom and sat at my desk, but without Amanda to hook my attention to, the room felt baggy. I worried, before the teacher had even called her absent, that she would not be back.

A special assembly was called. Our headmistress, Sister Brennan, announced to the school that Amanda had run away from home with her brother, a high school dropout who worked at Marshall Field's, and several stolen credit cards. As Sister Brennan spoke, there was a vast stirring around me, like on the day when we learned that Melissa Shay, two years below me with long gold braids, had died of leukemia during summer vacation. This stir was laced with delight, a jittery pleasure at news so shocking that it briefly banished all traces of normal life. I twisted around with the other girls, exchanging pantomimed amazement. It comforted me to feel like one of them, to pretend this news of Amanda meant no more to me than a shorter math class.

After that, I couldn't concentrate. I felt physical pain in my stomach and arms as I walked through the doors of Sacred Heart, this place Amanda had discarded. She'd left me behind with the rest: Father Damian in his robes, the old chalkboards and desks, the solemn chapel with its stink of damp stone and old lint, its stale echoes of the same words endlessly repeated. As Father Damian lectured to us on Amanda's sin, I noticed how the clerical collar squashed and wrinkled his neck, so it looked like a turkey's, how his eyes were thick and clouded as fingernails. I looked at Jesus and saw, where His crossed ankles should have been, the neatly folded drumsticks on a roasting chicken. I stopped looking at Him.

What compelled me instead was her desk. For weeks and weeks

—who knew how long?—Amanda had sat there, twirling her pen against her cheek and planning her escape. After school sometimes, when the shadowy halls had emptied, I would sit in her chair and feel the ring of her absence around me. I opened the desk and fingered her chewed pencils, the grimy stub of her eraser, a few haphazard notes she had taken in class. One by one I took these items home with me, lined them carefully along my windowsill, and watched them as I went to sleep. I imagined Amanda and her brother padding over thick dunes of sand, climbing the turrets of castles. In my thoughts this brother bore a striking resemblance to Jesus. As for Amanda, she grew more unearthly with each day, until what amazed me was less the fact that she had vanished than that I had ever been able to see her—touch her—in the first place.

One night, when my mother had gone to a meeting and Julius was reading in the den, I took a razor blade from the pack he kept in the medicine cabinet. I held it between my fingers and carried it to my bedroom, where I sat on the edge of my bed and took off my sweater. I was still wearing my school jumper with the short-sleeved blouse underneath, and I placed a pillow across my lap and lay my bare arm over it. My forearm was white as milk, smooth, and full of pale blue snaking veins. I touched it with the blade and found that I was terrified. I looked around at my childhood bears, my bubbling aquarium, and my ballerina posters. They were someone else's— a girl whose idea of mischief had been chasing those fish through their tank with her wet arm, trying to snatch their slippery tails. For a moment I felt her horror at what I was about to do, and it made me pause. But I had to do something. This was all I could think of.

Gently but steadily, I sank one corner of the blade into the skin halfway between my elbow and wrist. The pain made tears rush to my eyes, and my nose began to run. I heard an odd humming noise but continued cutting, determined not to be a baby, set on being as fierce with myself as I'd seen Amanda be. The razor went deeper than the pin had. For a moment the cut sat bloodless on my arm— for an instant—and then, like held breath, blood rose from it suddenly and soaked the white pillowcase. This happened so fast that at first I was merely astonished, as though I were watching a dazzling science film. Then I grew dizzy and frightened by the mess, this abundance of sticky warmth I could not contain.

I'd done something wrong, that was obvious. From the kitchen I heard the kettle boil, then the creak of Julius's chair as he rose to take it off the stove. I wished my mother were home. I tried to go to Julius and ask for help, but my arm felt so damaged, sending blood wherever I looked, and I couldn't seem to lift it.

"Julius?" I called. The name sounded unfamiliar, and it struck me that I hadn't said it aloud in nearly a year. The kettle was still whistling, and he didn't hear me.

"Dad!" I hollered, and it sounded even stranger than "Julius" had.

From the next room I heard the stillness of a pause. "Dad!" I called again. The wet warmth was soaking through to my legs, and I felt lightheaded. As I leaned back and shut my eyes, I remembered the Devil's Paint Pots with their wisps of steam, the man beside me on a donkey. Then I heard the door to my room burst open.

I was shivering. My teeth knocked together so hard that I bit my tongue. Julius wrapped me in the fox-fur coat and carried me to the car. I fell asleep before we reached it.

At the hospital they stitched my arm and wrapped it in white gauze. They hung it in a sling of heavy fabric, and despite my shock over what I'd done to myself, I couldn't help anticipating the stir my sling would cause in homeroom. Julius spoke to my mother on the phone. I could tell she was frantic, but Julius stayed calm throughout.

When we were ready to go, he held up the coat. It was squashed and matted, covered with blood. I thought with satisfaction that I had ruined it for good.

"I think we can clean it," said Julius, glancing at me. He was a big man with olive skin and hair that shone like plastic. Each mark of the comb was visible on his head. I knew why my mother loved him, then—he was the sort of man who stayed warm when it was cold out, who kept important tickets and slips of paper inside his wallet until you needed them. The coat looked small in his hands. Julius held it a moment, looking at the matted fur. Stubbornly I shook my head. I hated that coat, and it wasn't going to change in a minute.

To my surprise, Julius began to laugh. His wide, wet lips parted in a grin, and a loud chuckle shook him. I smiled tentatively back. Then Julius stuffed the coat into the white cylinder of the hospital garbage can. "What the hell," he said, still laughing as the silver flap moved back into place. "What the hell." Then he took my hand and walked me back to the parking lot.

Months later, in early summer, Sacred Heart and St. Peter's joined forces to give their annual formal dance. I was invited by Michael McCarty, a handsome, sullen boy with bright blue eyes, who had the habit of flicking the hair from his face more often than necessary. He seemed as frightened as I was, so I said yes.

I needed white shoes. After school one afternoon in our last week of classes, I went to a large discount shoestore downtown. I walked through the door and shut my eyes in disbelief.

Amanda was seated on a small stool, guiding a woman's foot into a green high-heel. There were crumpled tissue papers around her. I noticed her hair was longer now, and she was not so thin as before.

I had an urge to duck back out the door before she saw me. Although I hardly thought about Amanda anymore, I still clung to the vague belief that she had risen above the earth and now lived among those fat, silvery clouds I'd seen from airplane windows. What I felt, seeing her, was a jolt of disappointment.

"Amanda," I said.

She twisted around to look at me, squinting without recognition. Her confusion shocked me: for all the time I'd spent thinking of Amanda, she had barely known who I was.

"Oh yeah," she said, smiling now. "Sacred Heart."

She told me to wait while she finished with her customer, and I went to look for my shoes. I picked white satin with tiny pearl designs sewn on top. I brought them to the cash register, where Amanda was waiting, and she rang them up.

"Where do you go to school?" I asked.

She named a large public school and said she liked it better there. Her fingers moved rapidly over the keys.

Lowering my voice, I asked, "Where did you go?"

Amanda flipped open the cash drawer and counted out my change, mouthing the numbers. "Hawaii," she said, handing me the bills.

"Hawaii?" It was not what I'd imagined.

My mind filled with a vision of grass skirts, flower necklaces, and tropical drinks crowded with umbrellas and canned cherries. Julius had been there, and this was how he'd described it.

"We were there two weeks," Amanda said. "Then my dad came

and got us." She did not sound ashamed of this in the least. As she handed me my box in its plastic bag, she said, "He came all the way over, he had to. Or else we would've stayed forever."

Amanda closed the register drawer and walked me out to the street. The day was warm, and we both wore short sleeves. Her arms were smooth and lightly tanned. On my own arm, the scar was no more than a thin pink line.

We stood a moment in silence, and then Amanda kissed me goodbye on the cheek. I caught her smell—the warm, bready smell that comes from inside people's clothes. She waved from the door of the shoestore, then went back inside.

I felt a sudden longing not to move from that spot. I could feel where her arms had pressed, where her hands had touched my neck. The smell was still there, warm and rich like the odor a lawn gives off after hours of sunlight. I tried to spot Amanda through the store windows, but sunlight hit the glass so that I couldn't see beyond it.

Finally I began to walk, swinging my bag of shoes. I breathed deeply, inhaling the last of her smell, but it lingered, and after several more blocks I realized that what I smelled was not Amanda. It was myself, and this day of early summer—the fresh, snarled leaves and piles of sunlit dirt. I was almost fifteen years old.

EMERALD CITY

Rory knew before he came to New York what sort of life he would have. He'd read about it in novels by hip young authors who lived there. He saw the apartment, small but high-ceilinged, a tall, sooty window with a fire escape twisting past a chemical-pink sky. Nights in frantic clubs, mornings hunched over coffee in the East Village, warming his hands on the cup, black pants, black turtleneck, pointed black boots. He'd intended to snort cocaine, but by the time he arrived, that was out. He drank instead.

He was a photographer's assistant, loading cameras all day, holding up light meters, waving Polaroids until they were dry enough to tear open. As he watched the models move, he sometimes worried he was still too California. What could you do with sandy blond hair, cut it off? Short hair was on the wane, at least for men.

So there it hung, golden, straight as paper, reminiscent of beaches he'd never seen, being as he was from Chicago (in Chicago there was the lake, but that didn't count). His other option was to gain or lose some weight, but the starved look had lost its appeal—any suggestion of illness was to be avoided. Beefy was the way to go; not fat, just a classic paunch above the belt. But no matter how much Rory ate, he stayed exactly the same. He took up smoking instead, although it burned his throat.

Rory stubbed out his cigarette and checked to make sure the lights were off in the darkroom. He was always the last to leave; his boss, Vesuvi, would hand him the camera as soon as the last shot was done and then swan out through the sea of film containers, plastic cups, and discarded sheets of backdrop paper. Vesuvi was one of those people who always had somewhere to go. He was blessed with a marvelous paunch, which Rory tried not to admire too openly. He didn't want Vesuvi to get the wrong idea.

Rory swept the debris into bags, then he turned out the lights, locked up the studio, and headed down to the street. Twilight was his favorite hour—metal gates sliding down over storefronts, newspapers whirling from the sidewalk into the sky, an air of promise and abandonment. This was the way he'd expected New York to look, and he was thrilled when the city complied.

He took the subway uptown to visit Stacey, a failing model whom he adored against all reason. Stacey—when girls with names like Zane and Anouschka and Brid regularly slipped him their phone numbers during shoots. Stacey refused to change her name. "If I make it," she said, "they'll be happy to call me whatever." She never acknowledged that she was failing, though it was obvious. Rory longed to bring it up, to talk it over with her, but he was afraid to.

Stacey lay on her bed, shoes still on. A Diet Coke was on the table beside her. She weighed herself each morning, and when she was under 120, she allowed herself a real Coke that day.

"What happened at *Bazaar*?" Rory asked, perching on the edge of the bed. Stacey sat up and smoothed her hair.

"The usual," she said. "I'm too commercial." She shrugged, but Rory could see she was troubled.

"And that was nothing," Stacey continued. "On my next go-see the guy kept looking at me and flipping back and forth through my book, and of course I'm thinking, Fantastic, he's going to hire me. So you know what he finally says? I'm not ugly enough. He says, 'Beauty today is ugly beauty. Look at those girls, they're monsters— gorgeous, mythical monsters. If a girl isn't ugly, I won't use her.' "

She turned to Rory. He saw tears in her eyes and felt helpless. "What a bastard," he said.

To his surprise, she began to laugh. She lay back on the bed and let the laughter shake her. "I mean, here I am," she said, "killing myself to stay thin, hot-oiling my hair, getting my nails done, and what does he tell me? I'm not ugly enough!"

"It's crazy," Rory said, watching Stacey uneasily. "He's out of his mind."

She sat up and rubbed her eyes. She looked slaphappy, the way she looked sometimes after a second gin and tonic. Eight months before, after a year's meticulous planning, she had bought her own ticket to New York from Cincinnati. And this was just the beginning; Stacey hoped to ride the wave of her success around the world: Paris, Tokyo, London, Bangkok. The shelves of her tiny apartment were cluttered with maps and travel books, and whenever she met a foreigner—it made no difference from where—she would carefully copy his address into a small leatherbound book, convinced it would not be long before she was everywhere. She was the sort of girl for whom nothing happened by accident, and it pained Rory to watch her struggle when all day in Vesuvi's studio he saw girls whose lives were accident upon accident, from their discovery in whatever shopping mall or hot dog stand to the startling, gaudy error of their faces.

"Rory," Stacey said. "Look at me a minute."

He turned obediently. She was so close he could smell the warm, milky lotion she used on her face. "Do you ever wish I was uglier?" she asked.

"God no," Rory said, pulling away to see if she was joking. "What a question, Stace."

"Come on. You do this all day long." She moved close to him again, and Rory found himself looking at the tiny pores on either side of her nose. He tried to think of the studio and the girls there, but when he concentrated on Stacey, they disappeared; and when he thought of the studio, he couldn't see Stacey anymore. It was a world she didn't belong to. As he watched Stacey's tense, expectant face, Rory felt a dreadful power; it would take so little, he thought, to crush her.

"Never mind," she said when Rory didn't answer. "I don't want to know."

She stood and crossed the room, then leaned over and pressed her palms to the floor. She had been a gymnast in high school and was still remarkably limber. This limberness delighted Rory in a way that almost shamed him—in bed she would sit up, legs straight in front of her, then lean over and rest her cheek against her shins. Casually, as if it were nothing! Rory didn't dare tell her how this excited him; if she were aware of it, then it wouldn't be the same.

Stacey stood up, flushed and peaceful again. "Let's get out of here," she said.

Her apartment was right off Columbus, a street Rory scorned but one that nevertheless mesmerized him. He and Stacey walked arm in arm, peering into the windows of restaurants as eagerly as diners peered out of them. It was as if they had all been told some friend might pass this way tonight and were keeping their eyes peeled.

"Where should we go?" Stacey asked.

Rory cracked his knuckles one by one. The question made him edgy, as if there were some right answer he should know. Where were the people who mattered? Occasionally Rory would be stricken with a sense that they had been exactly where he was only moments before, but had just left. The worst part was, he didn't know who they were, exactly. The closest he came was in knowing people who seemed to know; his roommate, Charles, a food stylist who specialized in dollops, and of course Vesuvi. Vesuvi was his main source.

They headed downtown, enjoying the last warm days of fall, the pleasant seediness of Seventh Avenue. They passed intersections where patches of old cobblestones were exposed beneath layers of tar, relics of another New York Rory dimly remembered from novels: carriages and top hats, reputations and insults.

"Rory," Stacey said, "do you feel more something, now that you've gotten successful?"

Rory turned to her in surprise. "Who says I'm successful?"

"But you are!"

"I'm no one. I'm Vesuvi's assistant."

Stacey seemed shocked. "That's not no one," she said.

Rory grinned. It was a funny conversation. "Yeah?" he said. "Then who is it?"

Stacey pondered this a moment. Suddenly she laughed—the same helpless way she had laughed on the bed, as if the world were funny by accident. Still laughing, she said, "Vesuvi's assistant."

At Stacey's suggestion they took a cab to a TriBeCa bistro where Vesuvi often went. It was probably expensive, but Rory had just been paid—what the hell, he'd buy Stacey dinner. Maybe he would even call Charles to see if he was back from L.A., where he'd been styling all week for Sara Lee. Rory didn't envy Charles his job, although he made good money; sometimes he was up half the night, using tweezers to paste sesame seeds onto hamburger buns or mixing and coloring the salty dough that looked more like ice cream in pictures than real ice cream did. Rory had been amazed to learn that in breakfast cereal shots it was standard to use Elmer's glue instead of milk. "It's whiter," Charles had explained. "Also it pours more slowly and doesn't soak the flakes." Rory had found this disturbing in a way he still didn't quite understand.

Inside the restaurant, Rory spotted Vesuvi himself at a large round table in back. Or rather, Vesuvi spotted him, and called out with a heartiness that could only mean he was bored with his present company. With a grand sweep of his arm he beckoned them over.

The waiters pulled up chairs, and Rory and Stacey sat down. Stacey ordered a gin and tonic. Rory could see she was nervous—the girls at the table were faces you saw around a lot: red-headed Daphne, Inge with her guppy-face, others whose names he'd forgotten. What distressed him was seeing Anouschka, a moody girl whose journey from some dour Siberian town to the height of New York fashion seemed to have happened in an afternoon. Once, she had lingered at the studio while Rory cleaned up after work, humming a Fine Young Cannibals song and flipping aimlessly through his copy of *The Great Gatsby*. "My father is a professor," she told him. "He teaches this book." "In Russian?" Rory asked incredulously. Anouschka laughed. "Sure," she said, curling the word in her accent. "Why not?"

Outside the studio, Rory and Anouschka had hovered uncertainly in the dusk. Rory was supposed to meet Stacey, but felt awkward saying so to Anouschka. Instead, he blundered forward and hailed a cab, leaving Anouschka standing on the curb, then paid the driver three blocks later and took the subway to Stacey's. He arrived shaking, mystified by his own idiotic behavior.

Anouschka had frightened him ever since; last week, while he was loading Vesuvi's camera, she had casually reported the numerical value of her IQ, then subjected him to a humiliating quiz on the Great Books. "Have you read much Dostoevsky?" she called up the rickety ladder, where Rory was grappling with a light. *"The Brothers Karamazov?* No? What about *War and Peace?*" When Rory called back down that *War and Peace* was by Tolstoy, Anouschka colored deeply, stalked back onto the set, and did not speak to him again. Rory felt terrible; he'd never read a word of *War and Peace.* He even considered confessing this to Anouschka after the shoot as she grumpily gathered her things. But what the hell, he decided, let her think he was brilliant.

Now Rory looked at Vesuvi sprawled amid the models: sphinx-like, olive-skinned, his close-cropped beard peppered with gray, though his wild curly hair showed no sign of it. He was short, and wore high-heeled boots that Rory found spectacular. Vesuvi was a man of few words, yet he often gave the impression of being on the verge of speech. Conversation would proceed around him tentatively, ready to be swept aside at any moment by whatever Vesuvi might say. Rory watched him adoringly over his glass of bourbon, unable to believe he was sitting with Vesuvi after all the times he had watched him glide away in cabs, feeling as if most of what mattered in the world were disappearing with him. Yet Rory wasn't entirely happy: everyone at the table was watching him, especially Anouschka, and he felt that in return for being included, he was expected to do something stunning.

He glanced at the next table, where conversation seemed more lively. It was a group of downtown types, the men like deposed

medieval kings in their bobbed haircuts and gigantic silver medal-
lions. During his first month in New York, Rory had gone out with a
girl like the ones at that table—Dave, she'd called herself. She wore
nothing but black: bulky sweaters, short loose skirts, woolen tights,
and round-toed combat boots. The thrill of the relationship for Rory
lay mostly in watching Dave undress—there was something tremen-
dous in the sight of her slender white form emerging from all of that
darkness. Once she finished undressing, Rory often wished she
would put part of the outfit back on, or better yet, dress completely
again and start over.

Vesuvi was eyeing Stacey. "You look familiar," he said. "Did I
use you for something?"

"Once," she said. "Four and a half months ago."

"Right, I remember now. It was that . . ." He waved a languid
hand, which meant he had no idea.

"For *Elle,*" Stacey said. "Bow ties." It had been her best job,
and she was crushed when the pictures the magazine printed had
failed to include her head. To use them in her book would look
desperate, her agent said, so she kept them pasted to her bathroom
mirror. Rory looked at them while he was shaving.

Vesuvi sat back, satisfied. The question of whether or not he had
worked with a girl always troubled him, Rory had noticed, as if the
world were divided between girls he had shot and girls he hadn't,
and not knowing which side a girl was on caused a cosmic instabil-
ity.

"You worked for *Elle?*" Anouschka asked Stacey.

"Once," Stacey said.

"So far," Rory quickly added.

Anouschka glanced at him, and then at Stacey, with the same
startled look she'd worn when Rory left her on the curb. He felt
guilty all over again.

"You must've worked for them, too," Stacey said to Anouschka, who nodded absently.

"I heard you got a cover," someone said.

"Yes," Anouschka said dully. Then she seemed to take heart, as if hearing this news for the first time. "Yes!" she said, grinning suddenly. "I am the cover for December."

Rory felt Stacey move in her chair. Anouschka lit a cigarette and smoked; exotic, dragonlike, her black hair tumbling past her shoulders. For a moment all of them watched her, and against his will even Rory was moved by a face so familiar from pictures. Never mind what you thought of Anouschka; she was *that woman*—you recognized her. There was an odd pleasure in this, like finding something you'd been looking for.

"When do you leave for Tokyo?" Anouschka asked Inge.

"Next week," Inge said. "Have you been?"

"Two years ago," Anouschka said in her heavy accent. "It's okay, but when you take the morning airplanes, you see the Japanese men are coughing their lungs into the trash cans. They smoke like crazy," she concluded, wagging her cigarette between two fingers. Rory listened miserably; poor Stacey was barely surviving in New York and here was Anouschka, who not only had been to Japan but had the luxury of complaining about it. He rattled the ice in his glass and impatiently cleared his throat.

Anouschka glanced at him and turned serious. "Still," she said, "the culture of Japan is quite important."

"The culture?" Inge said.

"You know, the museums and this sort of thing."

Vesuvi, who had seemed on the verge of sleep, roused himself and turned to Anouschka. "You, inside a museum?" he said. "That I don't see."

The girl looked startled.

"You must have gone there on location," he said.

"Not location! I went for fun. How do you know what I do?"

Vesuvi shrugged and sat back in his chair, his lazy eyes filled with amusement. Anouschka blushed to the neck; the pink tinge seemed at odds with her extravagant face. Helplessly she turned to Stacey. "You have been to Japan?" she asked.

"I wish."

"But Milano, yes?"

"No," Stacey said, and Rory noticed with surprise that her drink was almost gone. Normally one cocktail would last Stacey an entire night, her sips were so tiny.

"Paris?"

Stacey shook her head, and Rory noticed a change in Anouschka's face as she sensed her advantage. The others were quiet. Vesuvi sat forward, looking from Anouschka to Stacey with great interest, as if they were posing for him.

"You never worked in Paris? I think everyone has worked in Paris."

"I've never been to Paris," Stacey said.

"London? Munich?" Anouschka turned to the other girls, confirming her surprise. Though she didn't glance at Rory, he sensed that all this was meant for him, and felt a strange, guilty collusion with her. He saw Stacey's hand shake as she lifted her glass, and was overcome with sudden and absolute hatred for Anouschka—he had never hated anyone this way. He stared at her, the gush of hair, the bruised-looking mouth; she was ugly, as the man had said today. Ugly and beautiful. Confused, Rory looked away.

"So," Anouschka said, "what places you have been?"

Stacey didn't answer at first. She looked double-jointed in her chair, heaped like a marionette.

"I've been to New York," she said.

There was a beat of silence. "New York," Anouschka said.

Vesuvi started to laugh. He had a loud, explosive laugh that startled Rory at first. He had never heard it before. "New York!" Vesuvi cried. "That's priceless."

Stacey smiled. She seemed as surprised as everyone else.

Vesuvi rocked forward in his chair, so that his heavy boots pounded the floor. "I love it," he said. "New York. What a perfect comeback." Anouschka just stared at him.

It began to seem very funny, all of a sudden.

A chuckle passed through the group like a current. Rory found himself laughing without knowing why; it was enough for him that Vesuvi had a reason. His boss gazed at Stacey in the soft-eyed way he looked at models when a shoot was going well. "It's a hell of a place, New York," he said. "No?"

"The best," Stacey said.

"But she has gone only here!" Anouschka protested. "How does she know?"

"Oh, she knows," Rory said. He felt reckless, dizzy with the urge to make Anouschka angry. "You don't get it, do you?" he said.

"What can I get when there is nothing?" she retorted. But she looked uncertain.

Vesuvi dabbed with a napkin at his heavy-lidded eyes. "Next time you go to New York," he told Stacey, "take me with you."

This was too much for Anouschka. "Fuck you!" she cried, jumping to her feet. "I am in New York. You are in New York. *Here is New York!*"

But laughter had seized the table, and Anouschka's protests only made it worse. She stood helplessly while everyone laughed, Rory hooting all the louder to keep her in her place.

"That's it," she said. "Goodbye."

"Go back to Japan," Rory cried. He had trouble catching his breath.

Anouschka fixed her eyes on him. Her makeup made them look burned at the rims, and the irises were a bright, clear green. He thought she might do something crazy—he'd heard she once punctured an ex-boyfriend's upper lip by hurling a fork at him. He stopped laughing and gripped the table's edge, poised for sudden movement. To his astonishment, the charred-looking eyes filled with tears. "I hate you, Rory," she said.

She yanked her bag from under the table and hoisted it onto her shoulder. Her long hair stuck to her wet cheeks as she struggled to free her jacket from the chair. Rory thought of his high school lunchroom: girls stalking out mad, clattering trays, their long, skinny legs skittering on high-heeled shoes. He felt a pang of nostalgia. She was just a kid, Anouschka—so much younger than he was.

"Hey," Vesuvi said, standing and putting his arms around Anouschka. "Hey, we're just having a joke."

"Go to hell with your joke." She turned her face away so that no one could see her crying.

Vesuvi stroked her back. "Hey now," he said.

Chastened, the group sat in guilty silence. Stacey and Rory traded a look and stood up. No one protested as they slid their jackets on, but when Rory opened his wallet to pay for their drinks, Vesuvi winced and waved it away. Anouschka still clung to him, her face buried in his neck.

Vesuvi spoke to Stacey in a lowered voice. "I've got something coming up you'd be perfect for," he said. "Who are you with again?"

Stacey told him the name of her agency, barely able to contain her joy. Rory listened unhappily; Vesuvi said this all the time to girls, and forgot the next minute. It was just a pleasant salutation.

They left the restaurant and headed toward the East Village. Rory longed to reach for Stacey's hand, but she seemed far away from him now, lost in her thoughts. Outside a market, a boy was perched on a stool cutting the heads off beans. A barber swept thick tufts of dark hair into one corner of his shop. From an overhead window came music, and Rory craned his neck to catch a glimpse of someone's arm, a lighted cigarette. The familiarity of it all was sweet and painful to him. He searched the dark shopfronts for something, some final thing at the core of everything else, but he found just his own reflection and Stacey's. Their eyes met in the glass, then flicked away. And it struck him that this was New York: a place that glittered from a distance even when you reached it.

They climbed the four flights of steps to Rory's apartment. A slit of light shone under the door, which meant Charles was back. They found him standing at the kitchen table, wiping a slab of red meat with a paper towel. He had a blowtorch plugged into the wall, and a dismantled smoke alarm lay at his feet.

"You poor thing," Stacey said, kissing him on the cheek. "You never stop working."

Charles's mouth was like a cat's, small and upturned at the corners. It made him seem happy even when he wasn't. "Meat is my weak point," he said. "I've got a job tomorrow doing steak."

He was prematurely balding, and Rory admired the look of hardship and triumph this gave him. Lately he'd searched his own hairline for signs of recession, but the blond surfer's mane seemed even more prolific. Most cruel of all, it was Charles who'd been born and raised in Santa Cruz.

"Here goes," Charles said, firing up the blowtorch. They watched as he moved the flame slowly over the meat, back and forth as if he were mowing a lawn. Its surface turned a pale gray. When the entire side was done, he flipped the steak over and lightly cooked its other side.

"Ugh," said Stacey. "It's still completely raw."

"Wait," Charles said.

He held a long metal spit to the flame until it glowed red. Then he pressed the spit to the meat. There was a hiss, a smell of cooking, and when he lifted the spit, a long black stripe branded the steak. He heated the spit several more times and pressed it to the meat at parallel intervals. Soon it was indistinguishable from a medium-rare steak straight off the grill. Rory felt an irrational surge of appetite, a longing to eat the meat in spite of knowing it was raw and cold.

Stacey opened the refrigerator. Rory always kept a supply of Cokes for her in there; Diet, of course, but also some regulars in case she had earned one that day and not yet rewarded herself. To his surprise, she pulled out a can of regular now.

"What the hell," she said. "I mean, really, what difference does it make?"

Rory stared at her. She had never said anything like this before. "What about Vesuvi?" he asked, regretting it even as he spoke.

"Vesuvi won't hire me. You know it perfectly well."

She was smiling at him, and Rory felt as if she had peered into the lying depths of his soul. "Vesuvi doesn't know shit," he said, but it sounded lame even to himself.

Stacey slid open the window and climbed out onto the fire escape. The sky was a strange, sulfurous yellow—beautiful, yet seemingly disconnected from nature. The shabby tree behind Rory's building was empty of leaves, and made a pattern of cracked glass against the sky. Stacey drank her Coke in tiny, careful sips. Rory stood helplessly inside the window, watching her. He needed to say something to her, he knew that, but he wasn't sure how.

He shook a cigarette from his pack and placed it in his mouth. Charles was working on a second steak. "By the way," Charles said, pointing with his chin at a spot near Rory's head, "I baked us a cake —a real one."

Rory turned in surprise and lifted a plate from above the refrigerator. It was a tall, elegant cake with giant dollops of whipped cream along its edges. "Charles," Rory said, confused, "haven't you been doing this all week?"

"Yeah," Charles said, "but always for strangers. And never to eat."

He bent over the steak, his blowtorch hissing on the damp meat. He looked embarrassed, as if his preference for real cake were a weakness he rarely confided. Charles's honesty shamed Rory—he said what he felt, not caring how it sounded.

Rory climbed out the window and sat beside Stacey. The bars of the fire escape felt cold through his jeans. Stacey held her Coke in one hand and took Rory's hand in the other. They looked at the yellow sky and held hands tightly, as if something were about to happen.

Rory's heart beat quickly. "So maybe it doesn't work," he said. "The modeling. Maybe that just won't happen."

He searched her face for some sign of surprise, but there was none. She watched him calmly, and for the first time Rory felt that Stacey was older than he, that her mind contained things he knew nothing of. She stood up and handed her Coke to Rory. Then she grasped the railing of the fire escape and lifted her body into a handstand. Rory held his breath, watching in alarmed amazement as the slender wand of her body swayed against the yellow sky. She had no trouble balancing, and hovered there for what seemed a long time before finally bending at the waist, lowering her feet, and standing straight again.

"If it doesn't work," she said, "then I'll see the world some other way."

She took Rory's face in her hands and kissed him on the mouth —hard, with the fierce, tender urgency of someone about to board a train. Then she turned and looked at the sky. Rory stared at her, oddly frightened to think that she would do it, she would find some way. He pictured Stacey in a distant place, looking back on him, on this world of theirs as if it were a bright, glittering dream she had once believed in.

"Take me with you," he said.

THE STYLIST

When they finally reach the dunes, Jann, the photographer, opens a silver umbrella. This is the last shot of the day. The light is rich and slanted. Around them the sand lies in sparkling heaps, like piles of glass silt.

A girl toes the sand. She wears a short cotton skirt, a loose T-shirt. A few feet away from her the stylist pokes through a suitcase filled with designer bathing suits. The stylist's name is Bernadette. She's been doing this for years.

"Here," she says, handing the girl a bikini. It is made of shiny red material. The girl glances at Jann, who is busy loading his camera. She slips her underpants from beneath the skirt and pulls on the bathing-suit bottom. She is not close to twenty yet.

"Is this the cover shot?" asks the girl, whose name is Alice. Each time she's in a shot she asks this question.

"Where were you two months ago?" the stylist says.

"What do you mean?" Alice's face is diamond-shaped. Her eyes are filled with gold.

"I mean where were you two months ago?" Bernadette asks again.

"I was home. They hadn't found me yet."

"Home is where?"

"Rockford, Illinois."

"Cover shot or not," Bernadette tells the girl, "it seems to me you aren't doing too badly."

This takes Alice by surprise. Her mouth opens as if to answer, but instead she turns away and lifts the T-shirt over her head. There is something despairing in the movement of her shoulders. She covers each of her small breasts with half of the red bathing-suit top. Bernadette ties the straps. Alice stares for a moment at the waves, which are pale blue and disorderly.

"Where are we again?" she asks.

"Lamu," says Bernadette.

Hair and Makeup arrive, panting from the walk. Nick, the makeup man, begins to work on the girl's eyes. She hugs herself.

"Where were we yesterday?" she asks.

"Mombasa," says Bernadette.

The photographer is ready. The silver umbrellas are raised to gather the light. He holds a light meter to the girl's chest. Hair and Makeup share a cigarette. There are two other models on this trip, and they watch from a distance. The sea mumbles against the dunes. The girl looks especially bare, surrounded by people who are dressed. She is still so new the camera frightens her. Jann has removed it from his tripod and is holding it near her face. "This face," he says, pausing to glance at the rest of them. "Will you look at this face?"

They look. It is delicate as a birdcage. Jann squints behind his camera. The rhythm of the shutter mingles with the breaking waves. Catching it, the girl begins to move.

"There," cries Jann, "that's it!"

They look again. Bernadette looks and sees it, too, feels the others see it. In the way the light falls, there is something; in the girl's restless hands, her sad mouth. A stillness falls. She is more than a skinny young girl on a beach; she is any young girl, sad and long-haired, watching a frail line of horizon. The camera clicks. Then the moment passes.

Alice leans down and scratches at her knee. Bernadette looks at Jann and sees him smiling.

"Bingo," he says.

In town the wind blows, filling the air with dust and tissue candy wrappers. There are lots of widows in Lamu, old squat women who clutch their dark veils against the wind. In the market square they hunch beside baskets of dried fruit, seeds, purple grain. The air smells burned.

The group is staying in an old two-story hotel near the water-front—the sort of place that conjures up piano players and rough men toasting their motherlands. It reminds Bernadette of the hotel in New Orleans where she spent her honeymoon. Like that hotel, this place has ceiling fans. Last night she lay in bed and watched hers spin.

After dinner, Alice tells of how she was discovered. It happened at the shopping mall, she says. All the girls walked through. You had to bring snapshots. She had one of herself riding on her brother's shoulders. The two other models look bored with the story.

JENNIFER EGAN

Bernadette lights a cigarette. She turns to Jann, who is flipping
through a magazine. "What does this remind you of?" she says.

He looks up, his blond eyebrows raised. He is gentle and
brawny, like a Viking from a children's book.

"What does what remind me of?" he says.

"This. All of us."

Jann seems confused, so she goes on. "Have you noticed how no
one really likes each other?" she says. "We're like a family."

He is amused. He takes a long drink of beer and runs his hands
through his hair. "Speak for yourself."

Bernadette laughs and then stops. "What's holding us together?" she asks.

"That's easy," says Jann, leaning so far back in his chair that the
cheap wood creaks. "That's a no-brainer."

"Humor me," says Bernadette.

He leans forward, resting his elbows on the oilcloth tabletop.
The wind carries snaking bits of music in from the narrow streets.
The models have wandered away, and the room is filled with people
so black their skin shines blue in the light.

"We're on a fashion shoot," he says.

He rolls a matchstick between his palms and then waves at the
waiter for two more beers. Flies settle on the table's edge. He looks
at Bernadette. "To getting those shots," he says, raising his beer. He
sounds uneasy. Bernadette drinks from her bottle, letting her head
fall back. Her neck is long and white. Jann watches her throat move
as she swallows.

"To the hand that feeds us," she says.

Now the girls gallop over. They want to go dancing someplace.
In Mombasa there was a discotheque filled with young African
whores who danced languidly and waited for business to arrive. The
girls were fascinated.

"Not in Lamu," says Jann. "Remember, there aren't even cars."

Alice yawns openly, like a cat. Her teeth catch the light. She leans down and rests her head on Jann's shoulder. In a helpless, teenage way she has adored him from the start.

"I'm sleepy," she says.

Jann glances at Bernadette and pulls the girl into his lap. He runs a palm over her soft hair, and she relaxes against him. Her long legs scatter toward the floor. All of them are silent. The girl squirms and moves her head. At this hour two months ago, she would be kissing her father good night. She climbs to her feet. "Well," she says, looking from Jann to Bernadette, "see you tomorrow."

She wanders in search of the other two, who have left her behind.

"Poor kid," says Jann.

As they watch her go, Bernadette reaches under the table and touches him, softly at first, then more boldly. It's amazing, she thinks, how you can just do this to people. Like stealing. Luckily, the youngest girls don't know it.

Jann looks at her and swallows. She decides that he is younger than she thought. She sips her beer, which tastes of smoke, and does not move her hand. "What does this remind you of?" she says.

He shakes his head. Color fills his cheeks.

"Let's go upstairs," says Bernadette.

They leave the bar and climb the narrow flight of steps to the hotel rooms. Bernadette presses her palms against the walls. She is drunker than she thought. They pause at the top, where insects dive against an electric bulb. Jann hooks his fingers into the back of Bernadette's jeans and gently pulls. Desire, sour and metallic, pushes up from her throat.

"Your room?" she says.

Jann's bed is neatly made, its curtain of mosquito netting twisted in a bundle overhead. He goes into the bathroom and shuts the door. Bernadette stands at the window. There is no glass, just wood shutters that have been pulled aside to let in the night wind. A bright moon spills silver across the waves. Painted sailboats line the shore.

She hears the toilet flush and stays near the window, expecting Jann to come up behind her. He doesn't. The bed squeaks under his weight.

"You know," she says, still facing the sea, "this reminds me of something."

"Everything reminds you of something," he says.

"That's true. One of these days I'll figure out what it is."

"Any ideas?"

"Nope." She stretches so that her stomach pulls. "It must be one of the few things I haven't seen or done."

Jann is silent. Bernadette wonders if he has pulled the netting down.

"Well," he says, "then it shouldn't be hard to spot. When it comes along."

Bernadette lifts off her shirt. Her bra is black, her breasts full and white inside it. There is too much flesh. This has always been the case, but after a day of dressing girls with pronged hips and bellies like shallow empty dishes, her own body comes as a surprise. She turns to Jann. "I'll know when I've found it," she says, "because it won't remind me of anything else."

He is lying down, hands crossed behind his head. His photographer's eye is on her. Her body feels abundant, tasteless. She wishes she had left her shirt on.

"If you close your eyes," she says, "you won't know the difference."

Jann shakes his head. The ceiling fan spins, touching Bernadette's bare shoulders with its current. She goes to the dresser and finds scattered change, film containers, a pack of cigarettes. She takes one out and lights it. There are Polaroids: two from this morning in town, another from the docks. She finds one of Alice in the dunes and holds it up. "What do you think of her?" she says.

"Cute," says Jann. "Stiff, though. New."

"She has a crush on you," says Bernadette. "I'm sure you've noticed."

"Poor kid," says Jann. "Should be going to high school proms."

Bernadette looks again at the picture. Sunlight fills the girl's hair. The sand is pale and bright as snow, the sea turquoise. She longs suddenly to be in those white dunes, as if she had never seen anything like them before. She must remind herself that she was standing just outside the shot, that she chose the girl's bathing suit.

"Have you ever noticed how meaningful these things can look?" she asks.

Jann laughs. "Have I noticed?" he says. "It's my shot."

Bernadette flips the picture back among the others. Her voice goes soft. "I meant in a general sense."

"In a general sense," says Jann, "that's how they work."

The room is filled with stale light. Bernadette goes to the bed. It's amazing, she thinks, how lust and aggravation will combine to push you toward someone. She sits on the bed and then wishes she had headed for the door. She would have liked to make him ask. He would have asked, she thinks.

She stretches out beside him under the twisting fan. It reminds her of a scissors. They do not touch.

"So," she says, addressing the fan, "are you planning to cash in?"

"On what?"

"On Alice."

His arms tense. "Are you always like this?"

"You bring out my best side," says Bernadette.

She takes his face in her hands and kisses his mouth. The sourness wells up around her gums and teeth. She wonders if Jann can taste it. She presses her stomach against him and works the T-shirt over his head. Undressing a person is easy—she makes a living at it. Jann smells like the beach. His chest is nearly hairless.

"What's the matter?" he says.

His eyes look cloudy and small. He pushes her down and moves above her now, pulling off her jeans one leg at a time. She watches his arms, the same thready muscles and veins she has watched as he held his camera these past days. She probes them with her nails, leaving small white crescents. He doesn't protest. She has him now, she knows it. And yet, she thinks, what difference does it make?

Later, when they have made love and the sounds of the bar have died down, Jann and Bernadette lie still.

"You know," she says, "this room is a lot like the one where I spent my honeymoon. New Orleans."

"Honeymoon?" he says.

"Sure. What else was there to do in the early seventies?"

Jann says nothing.

"I was pretty then," she adds. "My hair was down to here."

She turns a little, touching the base of her spine. The skin is damp.

"You're pretty now," says Jann.

"Please."

He runs a finger down her cheek.

"Stop it," she says.

"How come?"

"Because old skin always looks tear-streaked."

"How old are you?" he asks.

"Thirty-six."

He laughs. "Thirty-six. God, what a business we're in."

Bernadette touches her cheek in the place where Jann's finger was. She presses the skin as though searching for a blemish.

"I've been a stylist for sixteen years," she says. "I felt competitive with the girls at first. Now I feel maternal."

"Sixteen years," says Jann, shaking his head.

"They're younger now," she says. "You know that."

"They get older, too. Think what it's like for them."

"Who knows? They disappear."

"Exactly," says Jann.

They lie in silence. Bernadette decides she will go back to her own room. Conversation is meant to get you somewhere, and she and Jann have already been and gone.

"You know," he says, "it's hard to picture you married."

"I hardly was. It lasted a minute."

"How did it end?"

"Christ!" she says. "What have I started here?"

"Tell me."

She narrows her eyes and sits up. With her toes she searches the floor for her sandals.

"You can't answer a simple question," says Jann. "Can you?"

Bernadette touches her knuckles to her lips. The door is ten feet from the bed. She wishes she were dressed.

"I got restless," she says.

"Restless," says Jann.

"You know—restless? I kept thinking how many places there were."

Jann laughs. "I guess you picked the right life."

"I guess so," says Bernadette. She fumbles for her lighter. "You know," she says, "you ask too many questions."

She lights a cigarette and smokes it lavishly, sending out plumes through her nose and letting the smoke roll from her mouth. She thinks how much she loves to smoke, how conversations like this would get to her otherwise.

"So," says Jann, as she stubs her cigarette into the half-shell ashtray, "were they as nice as you thought? The places?"

"Sure they were nice. They were very nice. This is nice." She waves her arm at the ceiling. "I've been all over the world. You've done it, too, right?"

"I've done it, too," Jann says.

She shrugs, then slides her feet into her sandals and lights a last cigarette. One for the road, she thinks.

"My only regret," she says, "is that I hardly have any pictures of myself. All I've got is the shots I styled."

Jann nods. "It's like looking through someone else's photo album."

Bernadette twists around to look at him. He has a sweet face, she thinks. "That's right," she says. "That's exactly how it is."

She stubs out her half-finished cigarette. She wishes she had left ten minutes ago. She will stay another half hour, she thinks.

She lies back down, her body facing Jann's. His shoulder smells faintly sweet, like beeswax. She places her palm on his stomach, but when she tries to move her hand, Jann covers it with his own.

"Of all those places you've been," he says, "which was your favorite?"

Bernadette sighs. She is tired of questions. Strangely, she cannot remember anyone having asked her this one before. Is that possible?

she wonders. Surely someone asked, surely she had some answer. She tries again to move her hand. Jann holds it still.

"I liked them all," she says.

"Bullshit."

She feels a surge of regret at finding herself still here, at getting caught in this discussion. Jann moves her hand from his stomach to his chest. The skin is warmer there, close to the bone. She can feel the beating heart.

"There must be one that stands out," he says.

Bernadette hesitates.

"New Orleans," she says. "My honeymoon."

It is the only place she can think of. She feels suddenly that she might begin to cry.

Jann lets her hand go. He turns on his side so they are facing each other. Their hips touch.

"It must be quite a place." His voice is gentle now.

Bernadette moves against him. She cannot stop herself. Jann takes her head in his hands and makes her look at him. "Hey," he says, "what does this remind you of?"

He is playful, teasing. A thin silver chain encircles his neck.

"Nothing," she says. Something is caught in her throat.

For a moment neither moves.

"Okay," says Jann, pulling her to him. "Here we are, then."

The next morning they stagger through the dunes, giddy with exhaustion. It is still early, and the light is pale, frosted. It bleaches the waves. Jann is unshaven. Bernadette can't stop looking at him.

They're late. The rest of the group mills restlessly near the shore, turning to check on their progress across the sand. The models' faces look ghostly in this bloodless morning sun. They will probably guess, thinks Bernadette. She hopes they do.

"It's strange," she says. "Going back."

"To them?" Jann gestures at the group. "Or back?"

"Both," she says.

Later today they will fly to Nairobi. Tomorrow morning, New York. Two weeks from now she leaves for Argentina.

"Everything fades the minute you're somewhere else," Bernadette says. It's a mistake to say these things. "It fades."

Jann switches his camera case from one shoulder to the other. The stubble of his beard glints with perspiration.

"Some things have to last," he says, grinning at her, "or there'd be nothing but pictures you styled and I shot."

Hair and Makeup are waving. The others stamp the sand with mock impatience. It is too soft to make a sound.

"They're not enough," says Bernadette.

"No," says Jann. "They're not."

She tries to catch his eye, but he is hurrying. He said it once, she thinks. But she cannot let the conversation go. "It's not enough," she says again.

They reach the group. Everyone eyes them alertly. Bernadette enjoys this attention in a shameless, childish way she cannot remember feeling since high school. There is something exquisite in being wondered about.

The first shot is of Alice. She wears a black one-piece, skimpy, woven with gold threads. It is Bernadette's favorite.

"Better on you than on me," she says, snipping a loose thread. The girl's breasts are so small that Bernadette must pin the suit in back. Alice doesn't smile. Her eyes are funny today, as though she hadn't slept.

Nick, the makeup man, can't put enough shadow on. "You're puffy," he tells her, adding mascara.

"Puffy." Bernadette snorts. "Wait twenty years."

When Nick is satisfied, Alice goes to the water's edge. The two other models flank her, their backs to the camera. Alice extends her arms slightly from the shoulders, a ballet pose. As Jann begins to shoot, she raises them slowly. Bernadette stands beside Jann. She sees a thin child, a body barely settled in its first frail curves. There is something yielding in the girl's face, something easily wounded. She is looking at Jann.

"More eyes," he says. "Make them harder."

The girl lifts her chin, sharpening the thin line of her jaw. Her eyes are bright and narrow. She looks at Jann and Bernadette with the sad, fierce look of someone who sees a thing she knows she cannot have.

Jann is excited. "Kiddo! You've got it," he cries.

She does, Bernadette thinks. In three years she will probably be famous. She will hardly remember Lamu, and if she runs across pictures of herself on this beach, she'll wonder who took them.

When the shot is done, Alice wanders to the water and begins to wade. She still wears the black bathing suit, and standing alone she looks like a teenager about to dive in. After dressing the other models, Bernadette follows. She and Alice wade together in silence.

"I want to go home," Alice says. Her eyes are red.

"Twenty-four hours," says Bernadette.

"I mean home home."

"Rockford, Illinois?"

The girl nods. "I'm lonely," she says.

It's amazing, thinks Bernadette, how the young can just say these things. How easy it is.

"We're in Africa," she tells the girl.

Alice shrugs and looks at the shore. Oddly shaped trees rise from behind the dunes. Jann is shooting again. The other models lie stretched on the sand.

"Home never looks so good as when you're in Africa," Bernadette says.

Alice turns to her, squinting in the glare. "What do you mean?"

"I mean you can go home whenever you want," Bernadette says. "No one's stopping you."

The girl fixes her distracted eyes on the horizon. The water looks thick as molten silver. It feels warm against Bernadette's thighs.

"And then you'll be home," Bernadette says.

Alice dips her fingers into the water and paints wet streaks along her arm. She looks disappointed, as if she had expected to hear something else.

"But now that you've had a taste," says Bernadette, "you probably won't."

She feels a moment of pride in the way she has led her own life. I didn't go home, she thinks.

"I bet I won't," Alice says.

Something relaxes around the girl's mouth. She looks relieved. It is hard to pass up an extraordinary life.

"Anyway," says Bernadette, "I can cheer you up a little."

Alice shrugs, clinging to her gloom. She is, after all, a teenager.

"That shot we just did—that one of you?" Bernadette says. "That was the cover."

The girl runs a hand through her hair. Her lips part, and her eyes fill with tears. She is trying not to smile.

They turn at the sound of voices. Jann jogs toward them with Nick in tow. They have finished the shot.

"I want to get one of you," Jann says to Bernadette. "I'll make you a copy."

Bernadette glances at Alice. The girl has turned away, and her wet hands dangle at her sides.

"Us three," says Bernadette.

Jann hands the camera to Nick. He goes to Bernadette's side, and she stands between him and the girl, one arm around each. She can feel the bones of Alice's shoulders, fragile and warm as a bird's. She brushes a few stray hairs from the girl's face.

"Smile," says Nick.

There is a stillness, the pause of a moment being sealed. Bernadette notices the breeze, the limp water washing her toes. She feels an ache of nostalgia. Jann's hand presses against her back. Between them all is a fragile weave of threads, a spider's web. Bernadette longs for this moment as if it had already passed, as if it could have been. Yet here it is.

ONE PIECE

My brother builds models for a hobby. From plastic pieces he makes ships and airplanes, racing cars, those see-through human bodies where you put in the heart and stomach and things. I arrange the pieces for him. For years we've had the same quiet days: lawn mower sounds, children laughing on our neighbors' lawns, faint noises of TV from where Dad sits alone in his study watching a game. Every year the models get more complicated.

Six years ago, when Bradley was ten years old and I was seven, our mother started the car to take us shopping. After backing out of the garage, she remembered her grocery coupons. We stayed in the car, engine running, while she went inside to get them. It was a hot day, one of those afternoons when bits of white fluff fill up the air and under everything you hear beating locusts. That's how I think of it now, anyway.

Bradley sat in front. While our mother was gone, he slid over and started fooling around at the wheel, making believe he was driving. The electric door to the garage was shut. When our mother came back with her coupon book, she walked through the space between the garage door and the front of the car to get to her side. She was in a hurry. She had on a straw hat, and her hair flopped out the front. Maybe because of that hat she couldn't see Bradley. Maybe she saw him and thought it was safe to walk there.

The car jerked forward and hit the door. You wouldn't think a person could be so hurt from a thing like that, but they said she had bleeding inside her. Sometimes I stare at those plastic human models in Bradley's room with all their different parts and wonder which parts of her bled.

I remember my mother like you remember a good, long dream you had. I see a beautiful shadow leaning down, maybe over the edge of my crib. I remember her singing a lot, silly songs when she dried me after a bath about friendly vegetables and farm animals speaking in rhyme. She was in the church choir, and we would walk there together through the snow on mornings when the sun was so bright I had to keep my eyes closed. I held her hand, and she guided me over the ice.

There's one time I remember most, like that part of a dream that keeps coming back. She was leaving for the airport, dressed up in nice shoes and panty hose, and I was riding my trike. I must have been four years old. As she walked toward the car, I rode behind her, pedaling faster and faster until I hit her ankle and tore the stocking and made her bleed. It wasn't an accident. I knew what would happen, but I couldn't believe it. I kept pedaling.

I remember the look on her face when she turned and saw me behind her. Her mouth opened, and she stood touching her hair for a minute. Then she leaned down and put her hand on the bloody cut. I cried like I'd been hit myself. When I think of that now, I still want to.

With Bradley in the car, maybe it was like that. I think about it.

Bradley likes doing things that are dangerous. Stunts, I mean. He's raced motorcycles and jumped from a plane in a parachute. He's run along the top of a train, hang-glided, sailed alone on Lake Michigan when a storm was due. I watched all of it. There's a secret we don't need to say out loud: having me there keeps him safe. I keep my eyes on Brad no matter how far away he goes, and I hold him in place. It's a talent of mine, I guess. A kind of magic. When our mother walked through that space, maybe I looked the wrong way.

The Belsons are coming to our house for a barbecue, and I'm making a pie with Peggy, our stepmother since last year. Outside the kitchen window Bradley pushes my stepsisters, Sheila and Meg, on the tire swing. Peggy keeps looking out there like she's nervous. Dad's beside her, chopping onions for burgers.

"He's pushing them awfully hard," Peggy says.

Dad looks out and so do I. Sheila and Meg are six and seven years old, Peggy's daughters from her first marriage. Dad smiles. "Brad's good with kids," he says, kneading the chopped meat.

"That's not what I said."

Dad is quiet. I stare at my blob of crust. "What do you want me to do?" he says.

Peggy laughs. "Nothing, I guess." She dumps her flour and

sugar mix over a pile of apple slices. "If I have to tell you, then nothing."

She sticks her hands in the bowl and starts tossing the ingredients. Her wedding ring cracks against the glass. Dad's hands are still, covered with bits of meat. He's watching Brad. "I trust his judgment," he says, but he sounds sad.

"Me, too," I add.

Peggy looks from one of us to the other and then out the window again. She shakes her head. I hate her at that moment.

As I roll out the pie dough, I hear that heavy thump of a person's whole weight falling. Sheila lies on the ground under the tire swing. Meg is still holding on to it, looking stunned. Nothing moves for a second but the tire, which sails back and forth, creaking on its rope. Then Peggy runs outside, scattering butter and juice, and bends down over Sheila.

Dad runs after her. He's a big man, gentle most of the time. But today his face goes red and his eyes look small and fierce as an elephant's. He takes Brad by the shoulders and shakes him hard. "Godammit!" he says. "When Peggy trusts you with those kids . . ."

"Stop it!" I shout from the kitchen.

Dad looks helpless and clumsy inside his body. He gives Brad a shove that knocks him backward onto the grass. Then Dad pauses, like he doesn't know what to do. As Bradley gets to his feet, Dad reaches down to help, but stops halfway. He comes back to the kitchen and pounds both his fists into the hamburger meat.

Sheila sits on the counter, sniffling, while her mother wipes Bactine on her skinned knee. Dad shakes his head. "It was an accident, okay?"

Peggy doesn't answer. She leans close to Sheila's knee and swabs it with a cotton ball.

"I'm saying he didn't mean it," Dad says.

"Of course he didn't."

Dad watches her and Sheila, like something is still not settled.

"I just saw it coming," Peggy says.

Sheila parades her skinned knee with its bandage and orange stain for the Belson girls, who are close to her age. Peggy lays our pie in the oven, and Dad puts on his goofy chef's hat as soon as the coals are hot enough for grilling. He and Neil Belson each sip a Beck's and argue over whether the Cubs will make it to the World Series.

I lean against Dad's arm. He has big, solid arms that make you safe when he hugs you, like you're inside a house with its front and back doors locked. "Well, look at you, miss," he says, pressing a spatula down on the spitting meat. "This one's got my heart," he tells Neil Belson, raising his Beck's. "Forever and always."

They both laugh. "Who could blame you?" Mr. Belson says. I pretend to rub smoke from my eyes, embarrassed.

Sometimes I feel like the simplest things I do—chew gum, cartwheel across the lawn, even bite my nails, which I'm trying to quit—fill Dad up with happiness. His eyes get soft, and I know no matter what I ask, he'll say yes in a minute.

"Do me a favor, baby?" he says. "Use your magic to cheer up your big brother?"

I try to. I offer Bradley my pickle and bites of my burger, even though he already has one. I tell him a few dead baby jokes, which are the only kind I can remember. But he bites his lips and stares at his hands like he's trying to figure something out.

"Is Bradley feeling okay?" Celia Belson asks Peggy during lunch. Peggy leans over and whispers to her. They give each other a look that surprises me, like they both know something they don't need to talk about.

"How about a game of softball?" Dad says, wrapping his arms around me from behind and speaking to the group. He has a good, warm smell of beer and bread. Dad likes games: football, soccer, Parcheesi. Tic-tac-toe if there's nothing else. Our mom did, too, and when she was alive they'd play gin rummy late into the night.

Brad says he'll sit out.

"C'mon, Brad," Dad coaxes. "We need your power hitting." He wants to make up but doesn't know how. His hands hang at his sides.

"No thanks," Bradley says. "Really."

I catch another fast look between Peggy and Celia. Brad sees it, too.

I sit out with him. I watch the rest of them play, and Bradley tears blades of grass in two and piles the pieces at his feet. Everything is wrong: Dad's shoulders droop as he stands at first base. Peggy scowls while waiting her turn to bat. Celia Belson keeps glancing over at us. I stare at each one of them the way I stare at Brad when he's doing a stunt. But nothing improves.

Sometimes I have these thoughts. I imagine walking onto a battlefield where men are shooting at each other, and making them stop. Just by walking out there, just by looking at them a certain way and holding my arms up. I imagine how quiet it would be, like a scene from a movie where something happens to hundreds of people at once. In my scene the soldiers drop their guns and slap each other on the back the way men do when they're glad about something. They look at me in awe.

"I'll get the pie," I tell Bradley.

I run back to the house and open the oven. The pie looks

delicious, sugar bubbling along its edges. The dish is hot. I hold it with the oven mitts and sniff the steam coming out of the top. It's just what we need, I think.

I hurry back up the lawn. Sun shines in my eyes, and I blink a few times because it looks like Brad is at bat. I keep walking, holding the pie without noticing where I'm headed. He looks mad as hell. His jaw moves as he grinds his teeth, and I wonder what they said to make him play.

Dad is pitching, his back to me. Only after he throws the ball do I realize where I'm standing. Everyone sees it at once. It happens both slow and fast, slow because there's enough time after Dad pitches for parents and children to shout, "Bradley, wait!" and there's enough time for Brad to get the most awful look on his face, like he's seeing the worst thing on earth and he can't avoid it. Like he's the one about to get hit.

I just stand there, holding the pie. I know what will happen, like I've already seen it.

Then Bradley is shaking me hard, so my head bumps the grass. "Stand up," he hollers. "You're getting everyone scared."

I'm dizzy. I smell baked apples and sugar glaze. I hear people shouting, "Leave her alone for God's sake!" But Bradley keeps shaking my arm so it tugs in the socket.

I stand up and push the hair out of my face. Bradley puts his arm around me. "See? She's fine," he declares in a thin voice. "F-I-N-E. Fine."

The group stands in a quiet circle around us.

Brad takes my hand and pulls me. "C'mon," he says. "You need some water."

I try walking, but something doesn't work right. My feet aren't attached to my body.

"Come on!" Bradley urges, pulling my arm. I look at his face and see how his lips shake, how wide and scared his eyes are, and I try my best to follow. But the next time he pulls I fall onto the grass and then I hear more shouting, Dad's voice louder than the rest. "You get the hell away from her!" he bellows, and that's the last thing I hear.

I have a minor concussion, which is mainly just a greenish bruise near my temple and a bad headache. I stay in bed for a week, and every day Bradley comes to the doorway and stands there looking at me.

"I'm fine," I say the second I see him. "Completely fine." He nods and looks at me like there's something he wants to say but can't figure out how.

One day he comes in. He sits on the edge of my bed and stares at my face. "How well do you remember Mom?" he says.

It's the first time he's ever asked me that. I tell him about the shadow bending over, the singing. I want to tell him how I hurt her with my tricycle wheel, but for some reason I don't.

"She was beautiful," he says. "Like an angel." Then he leans back on his elbows, looking tired. "Know something?"

"What?"

"Dad's probably told you. Probably a hundred times. But I never did."

"Told me what?"

"You look the same. Like she did."

He's staring at me. There is a bluish color around his mouth, and his eyes have that spooked look you get when you stare in a mirror late at night. I watch the sheets. "No," I say. "Dad never told me that."

I think of pictures I've seen of our mother and try to compare us. But I can't remember what I look like.

"You're the same," he says. "No joke."

I twist the edge of my sheet, shaping it into the head of a rabbit.

Brad clears his throat. "Dad says I should stay away from you," he says. "He ordered me. Grabbed my shirt in front of everyone. Like this." He leans forward and grips the top of my nightgown, pulling me toward him. I must look shocked, because he lets go instantly. "Shit!" he cries, shaking his hand like he doesn't know who it belongs to. "Christ Almighty!"

"It's okay," I tell him, leaning back against the pillows. But my heart is beating fast.

Brad pulls a miniature rowboat out of his pocket and bounces it in his palm. He takes a small, crinkled tube of glue and dabs some on two plastic oars. "Look, Holly," he says. "I'm sorry for that."

He carefully glues the oars onto the boat. I wish he would go away.

After a while Bradley looks up at me. "You were there," he says.

"Where?"

He's staring at me in a desperate way. And then I know where he means: in that car, six years ago.

"What happened?" he says. "I want you to tell me."

"I don't know. I can't remember it."

Brad narrows his eyes. "I think you do. I think you're afraid to say."

"Well, I don't." It frightens me to talk about it. I keep trying to catch my breath, and it makes me dizzy. Brad looks more scared than I am.

"You saw," he says. "You know the truth about it."

I know I should tell about the thing with my tricycle. I should say how the worst things happen sometimes on purpose but they're not your fault. I should say the truth wouldn't matter even if I knew what it was.

Instead, I just lie there.

After that day Brad makes sure we stay apart.

There's a wall between my brother's room and mine. If I listen I can tell exactly where he is, standing up or sitting down, whether he's building something or lying on his bed, looking at the ceiling. When he walks I feel the floor shake under me. I can almost see him, I guess the way blind people do. Sometimes I see him so well I forget what else I'm doing.

My friends call. There are swimming parties, tennis games, all the summer things. I hardly go. I stay in my room and listen to Bradley, the same as I used to watch him. When I don't know where he is, I start to worry.

One time I knock and go in. He's working on a model of the *Apollo 13,* building the launchpad. I start arranging pieces by their codes, E's with E's, G's with G's, different piles for small and big. I know how he likes them.

"That's nice," I say, looking at the spaceship.

Bradley shrugs. I look around at the planes and boats covered in shiny paint, the racing cars and station wagons. They hang from the ceiling by strings. "They're all nice," I tell him.

Brad frowns. I remember going with him parachuting a couple of months ago. It was windy, and I stood by the side of the runway with long dry grass whipping my legs. Bradley waved to me from the plane before they shut the door, and his expression reminded me of astronauts I'd seen on the news, just before they went into space. You could tell they knew they'd be heroes if they ever made it back. So when Brad came staggering toward me through the long grass, dragging the parachute behind him, I started clapping. He had a streak of dirt on his face and was limping. He stood there smiling at me like he hardly ever smiles, and I think for a minute he felt like he'd been to the moon and back.

"You know, I do this stuff?" he says, looking up from the launchpad. "And I have no idea why? It's like it's all broken, and my job is to fix it." He laughs like it isn't funny, just weird.

"I know what you mean."

And I do. But Brad shakes his head like I'm just saying that to cheer him up. He goes back to his glueing.

The Belsons have a summer house. It's right on Lake Michigan, with a dock and a little beach and lots of tall trees that stick out over the sand. If you climb high enough in one of those trees, you see a whole new shore with houses bigger than the Belsons' on it. Brad taught me climbing three years ago, before it got too easy for him.

"I'd rather stay here alone," he tells Dad the day before we're supposed to visit them. I'm listening from the kitchen.

The leather in Dad's chair squeaks. "Brad, let's have a talk," he says. "I think it's time."

"If it's about Holly, you can save it," Brad says. "She comes in my room, I can't lock her out, okay? There's limits."

"Not about Holly."

"I'm following orders," Brad continues, more loudly. "Keeping away like you said." He lets out two hoots of laughter. I stare out the kitchen window at the tire swing hanging in the heat.

"You think I'm dangerous," Bradley says.

"Now you're talking crazy."

"You think I'm one of those people who causes disasters."

"Bradley," Dad pleads. "Son, don't say things like that."

"And what if you're right? What if I am?" His voice is thin and high, a crying voice. "I walk in the room and Peggy flinches like I might hit her, and you know what? I want to! I want to beat the shit out of her, I'm so mad. Maybe it's true!"

"Brad, stop. Stop, Brad, this is nonsense." I hear Dad getting out of his chair. "We're spooked a little, all of us. God knows why." His voice is wheezy. "I want you to come with us to Lake Michigan," he says. "We need to straighten this out. Clear it right up."

Brad doesn't answer, but I know he'll be there.

During the ride we play twenty questions and license plate bingo. Dad starts a contest counting gas stations, and Brad wins it. When I look at Dad's face in the mirror, I see him smiling.

After three hours of driving we park along a shady road and cross the soft ground to the Belsons'. Bradley helps Dad unload the groceries and sleeping bags from the car and bring them to the kitchen, then says he'll go take a swim before lunch. Sheila and Meg want to swim, too.

"I can't take you now," Peggy says, chopping an onion for Celia Belson's chicken salad. "Brad, would you mind—" She breaks off, and the room goes quiet. Even the kids stop talking. Peggy stares at that onion, blinking at her wet hands. The screen door snaps shut as Brad runs outside.

"—taking them with you?" Peggy finishes, like nothing happened.

I'm so mad at Peggy I bite my own tongue. I stare at the knife she's holding and want to take a swipe at her arm with it. But when she looks at Dad, I see she's mad at herself, madder than I am, afraid of what he'll say.

"I'm sorry," she whispers. There are tears on her face, but it might be the onion. Neil and Celia Belson work hard at gathering their trash into a bigger bag. Dad comes over and rubs Peggy's neck. He tells the girls he'll take them swimming after lunch.

I follow Brad. Between the house and the beach are dunes covered with tough reeds that scratch your legs when they brush you. Brad runs over those dunes, letting the reeds whip his calves. He splashes into the lake and starts swimming.

He goes straight out. I keep my eyes on him until he's so small I wouldn't know it was a person if I wasn't already watching.

"Turn around," I say out loud.

But he keeps going. In a hurry I run to a tree we used to climb, a tall one that sticks out over the sand and has a few boards nailed to the trunk. Bark flakes in my hands, but once I reach the first limb, the climbing gets easier. I see him again, moving out there like a spider on a big gray web. The higher I go, the better I see him, and I climb so high that the ground looks miles away. The branches are soft up here, and I hear lots of creaking. I straddle a branch and lean back against the trunk. I keep my eyes on Bradley, holding him up.

Then I see Dad below me on the beach. He goes to the water's edge and looks out. After a while Peggy comes out and stands beside him. She's brought him something in a napkin, but Dad takes a bite and drops it on the sand when she isn't looking. They just stand there, watching the lake.

I let them worry. They deserve it.

Brad is floating now, staring up at the sky. I glance up, too, just for a minute, at the thin clouds overhead. When I look back at Brad, he's disappeared. I stare at the spot where I last saw him and hold my breath, letting the seconds pass until I'm gasping. Finally Bradley splashes back to the surface—a big splash, like he's gone a long way down. He starts swimming in.

When Brad leaves the water, we're waiting for him. He keeps his head down. Dad gives his wet back a clumsy slap, then glances at his watch. "You've been gone almost an hour," he says.

"I floated a lot."

"We saved you some lunch," Peggy says.

In the kitchen I pull Brad aside, where no one can hear us. "They were scared to death," I tell him.

"Were you?"

I shake my head. "I watched you from the tree."

Bradley smiles a little, brushes some sand off my face. "I knew there was a reason I kept on floating," he says.

That night, Neil Belson makes a bonfire. He gathers sticks and branches and dry grass in a pile on the sand. His girls drag over what they can, and he thanks them loudly and makes a point of adding it. Celia brings out the potatoes in their foil and special pointed sticks for roasting.

All of us gather around to watch it burn. Fire wraps the sticks and leaves and crunches them to nothing. It makes a sound like laughing. Mr. Belson puts one arm around each of his girls, and Peggy holds on to Sheila and Meg. She touches her palms to their hot faces. I lean against my dad. "Look at Bradley," he says, shaking his head.

Brad is on the other side of the fire, sitting alone. Heat twists the air between us, so it looks like water running. Dad stares over the flames and smiles hard at Bradley, telling him with his face to come over, that he's welcome with the rest of us.

Say it, I want to order Dad. Call over to him.

But Dad just keeps smiling, and when Bradley doesn't move, Dad looks down and smiles in that direction, like he and the sand are sharing a sad joke. Meg wanders over, and he pulls her hair back and wipes the sweat off her upper lip.

I stand up. So many things are wrong I can't sit there. I feel crazy, like worms have crawled inside my bones. I go to the water and let it soak my shoes. Then I stomp through the sand so it sticks to my feet and turns them into blocks. I look up at where firelight smears the branches of the tree I climbed today. I stare at that tree a long time. Then I walk toward the house, double back, and start climbing it from the side no one can see. I want to look down from above. I want to keep my eye on Bradley.

The first long limb is high above the flames and a little to one side. On my belly I slither along to its end and look down. No one sees me. Smoke floats past in a column. Bradley doesn't watch the fire, he keeps his eyes on Dad and Peggy and the Belson family.

Sweat drips down my face, and I feel it running inside my clothes. The fire makes a panting sound, but it looks smaller from above. Watching Bradley and the rest, I think to myself: How can I fix it? I remember what he said about the models, how they're broken and it's his job to repair them. One right piece, I think, and everything will turn good, like the soldiers dropping their guns on the battlefield. Just one piece. But what is it?

Then Bradley looks up. Maybe he felt me watching him. He doesn't say a thing, we just look at each other a long time, neither one of us moving. Fire lights his face and makes his eyes look hollow. The only sound is wood cracking in the fire.

I rise halfway to my feet and jump. I stay calm until the second my shoes leave the branch and I see the bonfire coming at me like a giant orange mouth. People are screaming. I hear the crash I make, and there's wild, rippling heat in my hair and clothes. Then I'm on the beach, rolled and pounded by a weight that is Bradley, pushing me into the cool sand, smothering flames with his body.

Everyone tells the story, how he pulled me out so fast the fire barely touched me. Like he knew I would fall, and was waiting to catch me.

"A premonition," Peggy calls it, narrowing her eyes with respect.

"Reflexes," Dad insists.

Bradley's stomach got scorched. Not badly enough for the skin to be grafted, but red and blistered where he put out the flames in my clothes. At Lakeside Memorial Hospital they wrapped him in white bandages and told him to rest. They said the scars might last. I think Bradley hopes so.

My hair got burned, nothing else. It's short now, and when I lie in bed at night, I think I can still smell the smoke in it.

Bradley has to stay in bed. I sit in a chair right near him. We don't say much. It's peaceful in his room, with the cars and planes and trucks twisting quietly over our heads.

"What'll you make next?" I ask him.

He looks up, taking in all the years of projects. "I might quit for a while," he says. "Try something new."

"A stunt?"

"That's old," he says.

I glance at the door and see Dad watching us, holding a deck of cards. I realize Bradley's talking to Dad more than me.

I have the oddest feeling then. I feel like our mother is there, like the four of us are together again in that room for the first time in years. As Dad deals out the hands, I see her, like she's sitting beside me: her dark waves of hair, the thin gold coin she wore around her neck, her cigarettes that smelled like mint. I remember her warm hands and sliver of wedding ring.

What I notice most, though, is how different I look. My hair is pale and straight. My skin is darker than hers, and a little shiny. I have freckles on my arms, and when I try to sing, I hit every wrong note.

I lean over to say this to Bradley. You were wrong, I want to tell him, you imagined that part. But there's a peacefulness in his face that I haven't seen since before the accident. He feels her, too, I think, and he knows she's not inside me. She's gone forever. But she would want us to be happy.

THE WATCH TRICK

Sonny drove his boat straight into the middle of the lake and cut the engine. They rocked in silence, the deep, prickling hush of a Midwestern summer. The lake was flat as a rug, pushed against a wall of pale sky.

The four of them were celebrating Sonny's engagement to Billie, a girl with soft hair and a Southern accent. She kept to herself, leaning back in a chair with her legs propped on the rail. She had met Sonny the week before, at a party before her own wedding to someone else. This turn of events would have been more shocking in some lives than it was in Sonny's; he was a man who lived by his own egregiousness, who charmed, offended, and was talked about at other people's dinner parties. Stealing a bride was right up his alley.

Diana watched Sonny measure, shake, and pour martinis with

the ease of a cardsharp shuffling. She was forty-two, with a worn, pretty face. Her husband, James, sat beside her, looking amused. He and Sonny had been best friends since the army. James leaned back and looked from Sonny to his bride. "So tell us how you two happened," he said.

Sonny just grinned, his eyes fine and vacant as crystal.

Billie swung down her legs and leaned forward, animated for the first time that day. In two sips she had finished half her martini. "Let me tell," she said. "I'm dying to."

On the night before her wedding, she explained, her father had thrown a party aboard an old steamboat. Sonny had pursued her, flirting openly whenever he found her alone, eyeing her from a distance the rest of the time. Late in the evening they were standing alone on the deck when abruptly he took off his gold Rolex, held it up in the moonlight, and threw it in the water. "Baby, when I'm with you," he said, "time just stops."

Billie narrowed her eyes as she spoke. She was very young, and strands of roller-curled hair spiraled like ribbons down her back. "I'm like, please," she said. "could you possibly be more corny? But"—and here she seemed to struggle, reaching for Sonny's hand —"it was like when you're half asleep and you hear voices, you know, from the real world, and you just think, No, I want to stay asleep and have this dream."

She paused and tried to catch their eyes, but James and Diana were looking as far away as possible. They'd been hearing the story for years in various forms—from the Hawaiian tour guide Sonny fell in love with while gazing at the view from Kaala Peak, threatening to jump unless she agreed to come back to Chicago with him; from the astrologer who had obsessed him from the moment she divined that his mother had been killed in a small plane crash when Sonny was five. This very boat—a 34-foot Chris-Craft flybridge—he had bought twelve years before in the certainty that he would marry a professional water-skier he'd seduced the previous night. That was Sonny: music, a few drinks under his belt, the light falling a certain way, and any pretty waitress might receive a declaration of love, an impassioned lecture on their two converging fates. If she was smart, she would laugh it off and bring him his change. Not that Sonny didn't mean it—he could mean almost anything. But his attention span was short.

"So we escaped in a lifeboat," Billie concluded. "Daddy was mad as hell." She grinned irrepressibly now, a young, mischievous girl whose life had taken a sudden turn for the thrilling.

"That's quite a story," James said, with a sly look at Diana.

Sonny mixed another round of drinks. It was August, one of those hot, hot days when the sky seems to vibrate. Diana longed to strip down to her bathing suit, but her legs embarrassed her. Veins had risen to the surface in recent years. These seemed more offensive now, in the presence of Billie, who had long, gleaming legs and knees delicate as teeth.

"I hope Daddy will forgive me after Sonny and I get married," Billie said, suddenly despondent. "And Bobby, too, my fiancé. I've known him since the fifth grade."

"Your ex-fiancé," James reminded her.

"Oh yeah," she said. "Ex."

James and Diana's friendship with Sonny had had its perfect moment twenty years before, in the early seventies, when Diana wore short polyester dresses and thick pale lipstick. Sonny would squire them from one Chicago nightclub to the next, and each time they went inside she felt they were expected, that the party could really begin now that they had arrived. In pictures from those days James and Sonny looked surprisingly big-eared and eager. They were type-writer salesmen for IBM, and had started a side business marketing inventions—a solar bicycle, aerosol tanning lotion—that failed one by one and left them nearly bankrupt. In the end James quit and went to law school; Sonny later cashed in on fast-food investments he'd had the prescience to make early on. But in those first days they'd been convinced success was imminent, and would wedge fat cigars between their teeth and talk about the good life. Diana pic-tured it coming suddenly and with violence, a shock that would leave them reeling. But like so many things, success took longer than they thought to arrive, and by the time it came, it merely seemed their due.

After a second round of drinks, Diana went down to the cabin. The sun hurt her eyes—it had been like that since she'd started research-ing her dissertation, "Crisis and Catharsis in the Films of Alfred Hitchcock." She had promised James she would cut down the hours she spent viewing, but lately she found that everything in her life—the telephone calls, the endless, hopeful pounding of their son Dan-iel's basketball against the garage door as he struggled to match his father, the bills and invitations—seemed like nothing but distrac-tions from Hitchcock's tense, dreamlike world, where even the clicking of heels was significant. Diana often felt weirdly nostalgic as she watched, as if her own life had been like that once—dreamy, Technicolor—but had lost these qualities through some misstep of her own.

James came down to the cabin. He glanced up toward the deck, smiling, and shook his head. "Nothing changes," he said.

"Am I crazy," Diana said, "or is it more romantic this time?"

"You're crazy," James said.

"I guess it's always romantic when two people fall in love," Diana mused. "Even if it turns out not to be real."

"Turns out!"

"Well, never was."

"It's been a long time since the last one," James said, washing his hands in the sink. "I thought maybe he was outgrowing it."

"Oh, let's hope not!" Diana said.

James gave her an odd look, then opened the small refrigerator and peered inside it. He'd been a star basketball forward at the University of Michigan, and still had the ropey limbs and urgent, visible veins of an athlete. Lately Diana had wakened sometimes in the middle of the night to find James's eyes wide open. "What are you thinking about?" she would ask repeatedly, nervously, though he writhed under her scrutiny. She was worried he was having an affair, or wishing he were having one.

"You know," she said, moving near him, "today makes me think of the old days."

"Me, too," James said. He was tossing things into a bowl: mayonnaise, ketchup, Tabasco, chopped celery.

Diana watched his face. "We've changed since then," she said. "More than Sonny."

"Let's hope so." James looked up, meeting her eyes. "How?"

"I'm not sure."

She had noticed that she and her husband were more affectionate in public than in private nowadays, as if the presence of other people relieved some pressure between them. "I mean, back then," she said, "how do you think we expected our lives to turn out?"

James picked up an egg and rolled it from one palm to the other a few times, then set it gently on the counter.

"We were kids," he said.

———

Years before, while she and James were dating, Diana had once been seduced by Sonny. At the time she was twenty-three and fresh out of Smith. Sonny didn't like her. She'd been trying for weeks to win him over, but he seemed hardly to notice. She and James were staying on Lake Erie at the house Sonny had borrowed that summer, and while James made crayfish stew for dinner in the main house, Diana brought Sonny a scotch in the cabin he used as a painting studio. He painted copies: Pollock, Motherwell, Kline, de Kooning—anything really, as long as it was abstract (he drew badly). He worked from small reproductions cut from the pages of books, and his results were uncannily good. They filled the walls of his Clark Street apartment, and first-time visitors were astonished by the daunting collection he seemed to have amassed.

Sonny surprised Diana that day by looking pleased to see her. It was raining, and while she shook the drops from her hair, Sonny shut the door behind her and lifted the drink from her hand. He sipped, then handed it back for her to share. "I'm pretty hard on James's girlfriends," he observed.

"I've noticed. Is that a policy?" She was nervous, and held the glass in both hands.

"I keep the boundaries clear, nobody gets the wrong idea," he said.

It took Diana a moment to understand. "God, it's not like anyone would," she said. "I mean, you're James's best friend."

"That's why it scares me."

He went to the window and looked outside at the rain. Diana sipped his drink, relieved it was only this he'd had against her, not something worse.

"You think I should relax about it?" he asked.

"Sonny, you have to promise."

She crossed the room and stood beside him. She had finished the scotch, and now she felt loopy, bold. Setting the glass at her feet, she took Sonny's hand. "Friends?" she asked.

He nodded, then shyly put his arms around her. As they hugged, Diana teased herself, imagining what it would be like to make love to Sonny. Then he drew back, took her face in his hands, and kissed her.

Diana was as stunned as if he had slapped her. Gently she tried to pull away, but Sonny was running his palms along her back and kissing her neck as if this were all something they had agreed on. She tried to take it as a joke. "I've heard of self-contradiction," she said, "but this is outrageous." Sonny didn't pause, and as the moments passed, Diana felt drawn in by his fierce arousal, by the very fact that something so unthinkable was actually happening. The feeling was not quite desire, but something like it. It held her still while Sonny eased her onto the concrete floor, pushing a folded rag behind her head. She was crying by then, and tears ran from her eyes into both ears. She pulled Sonny to her, hooking her fingers over the thick ridges of muscle along his spine. He felt heavy and strange in her arms. His belt buckle struck the concrete—once, then again, over and over again with a thick, blunt sound. She closed her eyes at the end. When Sonny was done he stood up, slapped the dust from his hands, and picked up his paintbrush. Diana touched the floor beneath her, thinking she might have bled, though there was no reason. She ran through the rain back to the house, convinced her life would never be the same.

But nothing happened. No mention of the incident was ever made, and Sonny never again laid a hand on her except in the most benign affection. Only one thing changed: he liked her after that. It was as if she had passed some test or—and she tried not to think about this—as if she were partly his. What troubled her most was that she couldn't forget it; not Sonny himself so much as the paint-brushes soaking in their jars of cloudy water, the rolls of unstretched canvas, each detail bringing with it an ache of longing that still haunted her sometimes.

When Diana returned to the deck, Sonny and Billie were on the flybridge. "This baby measures depth," Sonny said, and sipped his drink. "There's where you pump out the bilge."

"What's a bilge?" Billie asked.

She was wearing a captain's hat, and Diana wondered if it was the same one her son, Daniel, used to wear as a little boy when they took him out on this boat. He was Danny then, and although he cringed to hear it now, Diana secretly preferred the childish name. He would sit on the tall seat, the hat nearly covering his eyes, and swing his legs while Uncle Sonny let him steer the boat. Sonny always kept one hand on the wheel; for all his recklessness, he'd been careful with Danny. "Kid, I'm raising you for the fast lane," he'd say.

Diana went to the stern and gazed at the lake. She was jealous of Sonny and Billie, though clearly this was absurd—they'd be lucky to last out the week. Yet in a sense it was this she envied: the fantasy, its tinge of the illicit. She stared toward shore and tried to block out Sonny's voice. A narrow strip of land was barely visible through the haze, yet it seemed, for a moment, to hold out some whispery promise—tennis courts, gin and tonics, secret, sweaty unions behind flowerbeds . . . Lord, what was wrong with her?

When James came up on deck, Sonny pulled a bottle of champagne from an ice chest and popped the cork. Billie held the glasses while he poured, champagne spilling over her fingers and along the frosted stems.

"It's suicide drinking in this heat," Sonny said with relish.

James collapsed in a chair and set the bowl of tuna salad at his feet. "Make mine a double," he said.

"That's a bit morbid," Diana said, but he didn't laugh.

Sonny passed the glasses around. His white shirt was transparent with sweat, and through it Diana noticed the darkness of his chest hair, the belly rearing up under his ribcage. Today would be one more day in a long spree for Sonny, and she found this comforting. Somewhere, at least, the party never ended.

"James, baby, I toast to you," Sonny said, slinging an arm around James and thumping his back. He must have noticed James was down, Diana thought—Sonny was quick to notice things like that. "You ought to be reminded every half hour you're a saint from heaven," he declared, breathing hard.

"Should've married you, Sonny," James said.

"Bingo," Sonny said. "Would've saved us both a heap of trouble."

"Now, wait a minute," Diana said, laughing.

Billie watched with rapt attention, her legs drawn under her chin. "You-all must've had some nice adventures, being friends so long," she said.

"Adventures. Christ," Sonny said, flopping onto a chair. He turned to James and Diana and all three of them laughed, helpless at how many there were.

"I wish I could've been there," Billie said.

Sonny took her hand and swung it gently in the space between their chairs. His own hands were small and over-muscled, crowded with jeweled rings he'd smuggled in from somewhere. Billie ran her fingers over the rings.

A lazy silence fell, and they lolled back in their chairs. Diana reached for James's hand, pleased to feel his fingers relax into her own. She thought of the old days; stories they still told about parties that started calmly—like Hitchcock's movies—and then spun out of control. "Am I imagining it," she said, "or was life completely different twenty years ago?"

Sonny laughed. "Not mine."

"Nothing changes but your body," James said, patting Sonny's gut.

"I could have some fun in yours, that's for sure," Sonny said.

"It's not like you're doing so badly," Diana pointed out.

Sonny turned to her. "I mean, what does he need it for? Parking himself in that stodgy office?"

"I work pretty hard," James said, "believe it or not."

Sonny pulled another bottle from the ice chest and shot the cork into the lake. When James covered his glass, Sonny poured right over his hand until James yanked it away, shaking champagne from his fingers. Sonny filled each glass to the top, so it spilled in their laps when they tried to drink. His unflagging excess lifted Diana's spirits. She could already hear herself, weeks from now at someone's dinner party: "We were out on Sonny's boat. His stolen bride was there, and Sonny'd been drinking for days . . ."

"What will the two of you do after you're married?" she asked, unable to resist. "What kind of lives will you have?"

James stared at her in disbelief.

"We'll give parties," Billie said. "Right?"

"Sure, lots of parties," Sonny said. "Parties every night."

"I hope you'll invite us," Diana said.

"Of course," Sonny assured her. "You'll be the guests of honor." He waited for James to speak. "Come on, buddy. Crash

course on married life. Should we get a dog? One of those basketball hoops above the garage? Cheez Whiz and Ritz Crackers?"

Billie listened with a frown, her idea of marriage to Sonny having clearly assumed a rather different shape.

"Follow your instincts," James said mockingly. "You're made
for marriage, Sonny. It's written all over you."

The sarcasm caught Sonny off guard. He studied James. "So it's
that easy," he said. "And here I've been admiring you all these
years."

"You've kept that a secret."

"What do you mean? I tell everyone." Sonny refilled the glasses
and shoved the bottle back inside the ice chest. "There was a time,"
he explained to Billie, "when James and I were in business together."

"Don't, Sonny," James said. He hadn't touched his last drink.

"We introduced a few inventions before the world was ready for
them. Then James abandoned ship."

"The ship was sinking. I had a wife and a kid." He, too, spoke
to Billie, as if a word from her would determine, finally, who had
lived the better life. She looked from one to the other, flushed from
their sudden attention.

"Anyway, being a lawyer isn't so bad," Sonny said, draining his
glass and setting it on the deck. "It's just boring as hell."

Billie stood up and moved behind Sonny's chair. She reached
her arms around his chest and rested her head on his shoulder,
closing her eyes. Her long hair gathered in his lap. Sonny wound a
strand around his finger. James looked away.

"What's boring as hell," James said, "is hearing you tell the
same lies year after year."

Sonny burst out laughing. "Less boring than the truth," he
cried.

"What're you talking about?" Billie demanded, letting go of Sonny and turning on James.

James shook his head. Sonny continued laughing in a loud, forced way. Now Billie marched over to James and stood before him. "How dare you insult my husband," she declared, using a voice she must have heard somewhere and liked the sound of.

"He's not your husband yet, and I wouldn't be in such a hurry."

Sonny let out a whoop. "Bastard!"

"James," Diana said.

But James was looking up at Billie, who loomed over him now, hands on her hips, her pointy elbows shaking. "I'd marry him before you any day of the week," she said.

"No one's asking you to marry me," James said quietly.

They stared at each other, Billie in a stance of pure childish defiance, James with a kind of confusion, as if the anger he felt toward this young, beautiful girl were a mystery to him.

"I'd go back to my fiancé first," Billie muttered.

"Give that some thought," James said. "Because if Sonny still remembers your name next month, you'll have done better than most."

Billie hesitated, smiling uneasily. She looked unsure of what James meant at first. Then she said, "I don't believe you. You're just jealous."

James said nothing. He looked suddenly tired.

"And even if he used to be like that," Billie said more loudly, "I couldn't care less, because Sonny loves me." She turned to Sonny. "Right?"

But Sonny's eyes were closed, and he appeared lost in some private contemplation. Billie watched him, waiting. Finally he managed to open his eyes and look at her, squinting as if she were a piece of bright foil. "That's right, baby," he said. "It's different this time."

Billie held very still, as if waiting to experience the comfort of these words. Then she began to cry. Her shoulders curled, and she lifted her hands to her face. Diana left her chair and took the girl in her arms.

Sonny shut his eyes again. Sunlight poured over his face, and sweat glittered in the creases of his skin. He opened his eyes and looked at James. "I slept with your wife," he said.

Diana froze, still holding the sobbing Billie. Everything seemed to tilt, and a finger of nausea rose in her throat. "James, it was a hundred years ago," she said.

"I don't remember it," Sonny said, "but I know it happened."

James rose slowly from his chair, and went to the edge of the boat. He gazed toward the shore. Billie had quieted down and was looking with smeary, fascinated eyes from Sonny to James.

James turned and veered toward Sonny, who rose halfway out of his chair before James hit him twice in the face, knocking him backward over the chair and into the rail. Billie screamed and clung to Diana. Sonny lay with his mouth open, blood running from his nose.

Billie and Diana went to Sonny, took his arms and tried to haul him to his feet, but he shook them off and stood up slowly. His breath stank of alcohol, not just a few drinks but a thick, rotten sweetness. Drops of red bloomed on his collar. He hovered unsteadily, pushing the hair from his eyes. "I'm gonna kill you," he said to James, "I swear to God."

"Do it," James said.

Sonny came at James and attempted a clumsy punch, which James blocked easily. But Sonny followed almost instantly with a second, jabbing James high under his ribs, seeming to force the breath from him. Then again, in the chin, so James staggered backward.

"Stop it!" Diana screamed, and tried with Billie to come between them, but it was impossible; the men shoved them away and lunged for one another in a frenzy, pounding, grunting, as if each believed his own survival hinged purely on the other's annihilation. Blood ran from Sonny's nose over his teeth, gathering in the cracks between them. He choked and started to cough, then went at James again, slugging his ear before finally James caught him in that boxing hold Diana had seen on TV, when the fighters seem to hug each other, heads down, so neither can move.

A perfect stillness opened around them. Everyone seemed to wait. Diana noticed the whiteness of Sonny's cuffs, a scar behind James's ear from his basketball days, the slick, marmalade-colored planks at her feet. The world disappeared; the only sound was the men's breathing.

Finally James let Sonny go and waited, poised for a response. But Sonny was barely able to stand. His eyes were running—it could have been the sun or the blow to his nose. Diana had never seen him cry in all the years she had known him, and found it hard to watch. But Billie couldn't take her eyes away from Sonny. She wore a look Diana recognized, the sick, scared look of a girl whose mischief has gotten her in trouble, who suspects her life will never be the same.

Sonny went to a chair and sat down heavily. He picked up a glass and downed what was left inside it, then fumbled for the bottle. "I can't kill you, buddy, I just realized," he said, making an effort to smile. "I'd be too lonely without you."

It was not until James started the motor that the world seemed to move again. A wind blew, the boat shook, and Diana inhaled the smell of gasoline. From the deck she watched her husband swing the boat around, his knuckles on the wheel, the hollow of his spine against his shirt. She was afraid to go near him. Sonny hadn't moved from his chair. His head was thrown back, and under his nose he held a towel filled with ice Billie had brought him. One eye was already going black.

Slowly Diana inched toward James, hesitating behind him on the flybridge. He had not glanced at her once since the fight with Sonny, and she felt as if he never would again. Finally she went around in front of him and touched his cheek, which was swollen and bloody. To her surprise, James grinned. Diana studied him, not sure what this meant. "The good old days," he said, and shook his head. He put an arm around Diana, and they stood side by side watching Billie, who was hunched alone at the bow. As the boat thumped over the lake, she leaned forward, watching the thick folds of water peel aside. Her curls had vanished, and now her thin, straight hair whipped madly around her head. Diana had an urge to go to her, to promise Billie she would thank God one day that none of this had worked. But she doubted the girl would believe her.

More than a year passed before James and Diana saw much of Sonny again. By then Diana had earned her Ph.D. and was teaching in the Film Studies Department at the U. of I.'s Circle Campus. Sonny had grown even fatter, and his complexion was the color of raw oysters. The doctor issued continual warnings, but Sonny's only response had been to take up occasional smoking. Diana noticed that he flicked the cigarette constantly, so that it never had time to gather any ash.

"Remember that time I almost killed you?" he would ask James sometimes when they'd had a few drinks. "I should've let you have it—don't know what stopped me."

"Willpower," James said, grinning at Diana. "Pure self-restraint."

"Don't kid yourself, buddy. It was pity."

This was one story James and Diana never told at parties. Except sometimes the beginning, where Sonny made off with a bride on the eve of her own wedding. The rest they kept to themselves, hardly mentioning it, lest it take on that eerie power of old movies and faded snapshots, an allure against which the present day could only pale.

Now and then Diana still thought of Billie, who had gone back to her original fiancé and married him. Somewhere in the Deep South, Diana guessed, the girl must occasionally tell the story of her brief elopement with a madman. "It was terrible!" she would say. "It was something out of hell." Yet Diana guessed that when Billie looked at the familiar trappings of her life and recalled that strange day, she was sometimes wistful.

PASSING THE HAT

The first time I saw her, she was waiting in line for a chairlift. "There's Catherine Black," someone said. "Jack Delancey's girl-friend." I saw a tanned, buxom woman in her late twenties (the authenticity of whose breasts I immediately questioned), wearing a pair of skintight blue ski overalls. One strap ran straight down the middle of each breast. She had a wide, pretty mouth, and struck me as someone I knew without having to meet her: sexy and brash, filled with loud and abundant laughter, not afraid to drink too much. The sort of woman married men dream about, but who is rarely married herself. And of course, I disliked her instantly.

Jack Delancey was part of the crowd my husband, Ted, and I belonged to, young stock brokers and investment bankers and their pretty wives, all of us making money, having children, and intending to do a great deal more of both. Most of us had moved to San Francisco recently from drab Midwestern towns (Springfield, Illinois, in our case) and regarded our arrival here as a near escape from a disaster. We were giddy. While other people our age were protesting the Vietnam War and experimenting with communes, we were buying and redecorating vast houses, overextending ourselves on private schools, and throwing summertime parties in Belvedere and Tiburon, where late at night you were likely to be shoved, fully clothed and still holding your glass, into someone's swimming pool.

Catherine Black must have been at most of those early parties. I hardly remember her, though, except at one Ted and I gave, where she wore a white backless summer dress with a high collar. Her back was tanned and very smooth, the skin tight over her ribs so they rippled like a seashell. We were the same age, more or less, but she had that perfect seamlessness of waist and hip that comes of not having been pregnant.

"Charlotte," she cried as the evening wore on, "I've broken my glass."

She held it out for me, the long, thin shards like blades of ice. "I'm so sorry," she said, smiling drunkenly, then looked as if she might cry.

"It's nothing," I said. "Forget it."

I took the shards from her, but by the time I reached the garbage, I'd cut myself. Blood ran between my fingers, gathering around the nails.

I try sometimes to remember what dessert I served that night (my frozen avocado mousse, which sounded so awful and tasted so good?), or who told the funniest story at dinner, or whether anyone ended up pitching into the deep beds of ivy outside our front door. But I can't recall. Once I've released Catherine's glass from my bloodied hand, that evening blurs in my mind with other parties we gave—the living room crowded with laughter and smoke, the sweet odor of gin, our daughter, Jessica, pigtailed and barefoot in her nightie, proudly serving drinks. And here I am, fifteen or so years later, pausing on this foggy street while the black Labrador puppy I still cannot believe I own snaps at dry leaves. For years my children begged me for a dog, but I wouldn't allow it. I call her Rover, hoping irony will rescue me from self-contradiction.

It's nearly dark. Below me the bay is covered in fine, watery light. I've taken a break from emptying my closet, pulling out clothes I haven't looked at in years, clothes bundled in plastic. I'll send them to Jessica, back East, where she is a sophomore in college.

I was making soup for dinner once, and as I placed the pot in the sink and lifted its lid, Ted came up behind me and reached around my waist. The windows above the sink were squares of bright black, and steam clung to them like frost. As it melted away, we saw ourselves reflected in the glass. Ted kept his arms around me. We listened to the thump of Joel's and Jessica's feet above our heads.

"God knows what they're doing up there, the little hell-raisers," Ted said, grinning at our reflection.

"God knows," I said.

We rocked back and forth, watching the picture we made. Neither one of us spoke. Ted's heart seemed to push directly against my ribs, and with each breath his stomach filled the hollow of my back. Our life pulled in around us for a moment, a thing we could measure and hold. We had what we wanted.

Now I wonder why I remember that night. There must have been a hundred other times when Ted and I stood before that sink, endless pots of soup whose lids I lifted. We even made love on the floor of that kitchen once, when we first moved in—a sort of earthy christening. I know that happened, but I can't remember it. Instead, what comes back again and again is the two of us standing there, watching ourselves rock. And of course, I'm glad to have it. When it comes to memory, I suppose, we're all passing the hat.

Catherine Black and Jack Delancey were together two years, and after they broke up he married someone else. Catherine dated Chuck Peyton after that, one of the last single men left in our group, then had a series of shorter affairs with people I knew less well. When our friends Wally and Clara Davidson separated, Wally dated Catherine, and the rumor was that they'd been involved long before that. Clara Davidson disappeared from sight. People were cool to Wally at first, but it was hard to sustain—he and Catherine were everywhere that winter, giving parties, going to parties, having long, boisterous lunches in the ski lodge at Sugar Bowl, where Wally owned a house. Catherine had never looked happier, I thought, as if there were some thrill, some rarefied pleasure most of us would never know, that came of stealing a man from his wife.

I ended up in Wally's sauna that winter with a group that included Catherine, who wore a sparkling green bikini. Her torso and limbs looked stringier than they had a few summers before, and her skin seemed leathery from one too many Caribbean vacations. She was drinking a glass of wine, and began dipping her fingers into the glass and then flicking white wine onto the hot, dark stones of the grate. The stones gasped, and a burst of winy steam filled the room. We felt its tartness in our throats. My daughter watched, wide-eyed with amazement and delight, as if Catherine had shot columns of flame from each of her long red fingernails.

The next morning, after putting the kids into ski school, I discovered too late that I was right behind Catherine Black in the lift line. We both feigned delight at the coincidence, this long-awaited chance to really talk, then struggled to fill the silence.

"Where's Wally?" I asked as the chair lifted us from the ground.

"He went up early with Mike Minetta," she said. "I think they're skiing Siberia."

"Ted, too," I said. "They must be up there together."

The lift whispered along its track. It had snowed the night before, and beneath us the untouched hill was smooth and white as eggshell. The small trees buckled under their load, slim trunks bent. I looked down at Catherine's thighs, then at mine, pleased to find hers slightly thicker. Her perfume was strong for so early in the day.

"You've made quite a hit with my daughter," I said, groping for some topic.

"Really? With Jessica?"

It surprised me that she knew my daughter's name. "Oh yes," I said. "She thinks you're wonderful. She told me you looked like a movie star." My words amazed me—what compliments dislike could generate!

"God," Catherine said. "What do you know."

Without turning my head, I glanced at her broad, tanned face, the eyes deeply lined by now, the cheeks faintly shiny with makeup. It had been five or six years since I'd first seen her, waiting in line for the chairlift. It seemed to me she wasn't aging well.

"I like kids," she said.

"That's funny," I said. "I never liked kids until I had them."

"I've had longer to think about it."

This puzzled me. I had always assumed Catherine chose the sort of life she led; a taste for children didn't seem to fit. "Well," I said, "if you and Wally . . ."

Catherine laughed—a loud, reckless laugh that startled me. I felt I'd been caught in a lie, and blushed to my neck. "Come on. Wally won't marry me," she said.

"I hadn't given it much thought," I said, "frankly."

"Well, he won't," she said, lighting a cigarette with a slim, oval-shaped lighter, then snapping it shut. "Everyone knows that."

I watched her face arrange itself around the cigarette, as if every crease had been formed by this act. Strangely, I had an urge to smoke one myself, which I hadn't done since college.

Catherine wasn't laughing anymore, but looked as if she might start again at any moment. "It's funny," she said, narrowing her eyes. "There are things you're just positive will happen to you. Then there's that second when you realize, Jesus Christ. Maybe they won't."

She was watching me closely. Her eyes, I noticed, were bloodshot. I shifted the ski pole under my leg.

"Have you ever had a feeling like that?" she asked.

"Not exactly," I said, uneasy. "I guess I have most things I wanted."

"You're lucky."

I felt her envy, sharp as the tang of her cigarette smoke on the cold air. We were far apart, I realized then, and this filled me with relief.

Catherine flicked her half-smoked cigarette into a snowbank. "Of course," she said, "getting what you want is only the beginning. The hard part is holding on to it."

I was annoyed. "How do you know?"

Catherine took a while to answer. She seemed deep in thought. "I just know," she finally said.

As I head toward home, I find myself studying the neighborhood, now that I'll be leaving it for good. Houses have changed color again since I last noticed, houses whose hues seemed so indelible when we first arrived that the neighborhood will always look fake to me. Most of our friends have split up and moved; different cities, different countries, strange, unlikely fates. Someone told me Katy Alistair's daughter is a stripper in Guam; Joel's childhood friend Bobby Zimmerman was found hanging from a light fixture in the Tenderloin. But these are only the most dramatic cases; most kids have simply gone off to college, their parents divorced, husbands married to younger women and starting second families. I see young, strange faces through the windows of houses I've been inside so many times, unfamiliar children hitting tennis balls against garage doors. It galls me, how at home they seem. I have a lunatic urge sometimes to go up to one of those kids and say, "Understand something, junior: you don't really live here. Not like we did."

Two different families have lived in our house since we moved. The second, the Weisels, invited me to a dinner party several weeks ago. Against my better instincts, curiosity led me to accept. I wandered through the familiar rooms, remembering the paint samples and fabric swatches Ted and I had argued over—all gone, the curtains gone, the walls a different color, a vast Chinese urn where we used to put our Christmas tree. I could almost hear the scuttling of Joel's footed pajamas across the floor—those same boards! I searched the walls and corners for some trace of our lives, something left behind by mistake. But there was nothing. The house might never have existed before that night. As I ate my lemon mousse, I felt lightheaded, giddy, as if I myself had narrowly escaped the same oblivion. I drank another glass of wine. By midnight, I had to ask where to find the bathroom.

Catherine Black shot herself in the South of France two summers ago. People were shocked, of course, but less so than they might have been if she'd done it a few years before. She had gone, as they say, downhill, appearing more and more often alone, distracted, without the high spirits she was famous for. It was assumed that the men she saw were all married. I've tried lately to imagine the scene of her death: Was she staying in some man's villa? Aboard his yacht? Was it a fit of passion, or did she simply look up one day at the palm leaves flapping against a blue sky and know that it was time?

Rover and I take a detour and stop before what used to be my house. I almost never do this, although my apartment is only a few blocks away. But in two days the moving trucks will come and take me to my new apartment on Russian Hill. After so many years in the same ten-block radius, I feel like I'm leaving the country.

It's finally dark. The foghorns honk and call, sounds as familiar to me as my own voice. The house is a strange gold color now, the ivy overtrimmed, without the chaotic appeal it had while we lived here. It must have been the vitamins my children used to toss into that ivy each morning as they left for school (after pretending to swallow them) that made it grow so wild. Once, during a hard rain, dozens of half-disintegrated pills washed onto the path.

Rover pants quietly beside me as I watch the lighted windows of our old living room. Beyond the open curtains someone moves, and I wait, half expecting to catch a glimpse of Ted tossing a log on the fire, of Joel running past with a tennis ball in his hand. Or myself, reading the evening paper, drinking tea. If I saw us, I suppose I would believe it for a minute, as if those memories were still real, my presence out here the illusion. But as Frank Weisel moves into the light to adjust the volume on his stereo, I feel unexpected relief. I'm weightless. There's nothing left here—I'll take it all when I go.

Like most things that happen well after they should, my divorce from Ted three years ago was unpleasant. In one of many confessions I could have lived without, he admitted to having been involved with Catherine Black off and on over the years.

"How many years?" I asked.

"I don't remember exactly."

" 'Years' is not specific," I said. "I want a number: two? three? five?"

"Calm down," Ted said. "It was insignificant. You know Catherine, she was around. She made it easy."

"When did it start?"

"I don't know when. It was some years, all right?"

" 'Some' means a lot."

"It meant nothing, Charlotte," Ted said, growing frantic. "Zero. Nada. We were treading water, she knew that as well as I did."

"Probably better," I said.

Ted glanced at me, but seemed afraid to pursue the topic. I went on packing books into boxes; books from college, Book-of-the-Month Club books, so many I still hadn't read. I thought of that day when I'd ridden the chairlift with Catherine (six years before? seven?), and was appalled at what an idiot I might have been—how, that whole time, she might have been laughing at me. The thought haunted me for months after Ted had gone. But eventually I stopped wondering whether or not it had already started between them. How could it matter? What I felt on the chairlift with Catherine wasn't spite or cruelty, not even smug satisfaction. She'd been left outside my world, that was all. And from there she saw how quickly it would pass.

Back at my own apartment, I weave my way among packing boxes to the kitchen and pour myself a glass of Chardonnay. I call Jessica at her dormitory, and to my astonishment, she answers. "Sweetheart. How are things?" I ask.

She sounds breathless. I hear music in the background. "They're crazy," she says. "I've got way more than I can ever do."

I see her, brown curls dangling in her eyes, thrilled by the dire earnestness of her life. She hollers "Shut up!" at someone, and I hold the phone away.

"I'm sending you some clothes," I tell her. "That rose-colored suit, for instance. The suede?"

"You're giving that to me?" she asks, startled. "But you've had it so long."

"Exactly." I wait a moment, then ask, "So. What do you hear from your father?"

Jessica hesitates, for try as I might to make the question sound neutral, it is always tinged with my hope that she'll answer, "Nothing. I've decided never to speak to him again."

"He's visiting next weekend," she says.

"With Beatrice and the baby?"

"I think so," she says. "But Mom? How're you doing?"

"Just fine," I say.

"Had any dates?"

"Here and there." I decide not to mention the one last month who revealed to me, as we sat kissing on my couch after too much wine, that he'd been a Roman centurion in his previous life. "Actually, I'm going out tonight with Bud Templeton," I say. "Remember him?"

"Amy's father?" She sounds aghast.

"That's right. He and his second wife have split."

"You're going out with Amy's father?"

"Should I have asked Amy's permission?"

Jessica laughs. "No, it's just, I don't know. It seems weird, you and Mr. Templeton going out together."

I find I am at a loss. There is a pause before I answer, "Well, I think so, too, sweetheart. But that's what happens." After a moment I add, "I call him Bud, though."

"Well, have fun," she says, though I sense she feels the possibility is remote.

We hang up, and I go back to my closet to do another hour's work. I'm looking forward to tonight—I always liked Bud Templeton, though I've hardly seen him in years. I still think of him as the tall, wry neurologist I loved to chat with over plastic cups of wine at school plays. We would congratulate each other on our daughters' performances as orphans or lost boys, one eyebrow raised to show that, unlike some parents, we had this all in perspective. But perspective was what I lacked, it turns out, for my life had felt as permanent as childhood. I've even outgrown the clothes I wore as a young wife: summer suits, skirts below the knee, tall black boots—none of it fits; I've become a smaller version of myself, distilled from an earlier abundance I was not even aware of. I take unexpected pleasure now in packing these outfits away and stepping into a sleek, narrow dress I bought last week. I carry my wine to the window and wait, my face near the glass. The sky is clear and dark, the lights of the city trembling beneath it. As I watch them, I'm overwhelmed by a feeling I haven't had in years: a sweet, giddy sense that anything might happen to me.

Catherine Black. Sometimes I imagine she was everywhere for those years, quietly watching me live. Waiting—for what? I see us on that chairlift, our skis casting long gray shadows over hills like piles of sugar. Her skis were slightly pigeon-toed, I think. We're there, eyes fixed to the top of the hill, both counting the moments until we can reach it and ski away from one another.

PUERTO VALLARTA

On their last day in Puerto Vallarta, the fathers rented horses. Ellen's father let her come along, though she was only eleven and hadn't ridden before. She stayed close to his side, staring at the tin shacks and rows of hobbled corn along the back streets. Her father drank wine from a pig-bladder pouch and gave her a sip when she asked. It was sour and hot. He bought her a sombrero embroidered with green and pink flowers and placed it carefully over her head. Gradually they drifted apart from the others.

Ellen was rarely alone with her father. She and her parents had joined two other families in Mexico, and for ten days they all had descended in large, whooping groups over local cafés and beaches. Her father told jokes and chose restaurants, whatever people wanted. He was Master of Ceremonies.

"Aren't we meeting Mom for lunch?" Ellen asked when she and her father reached a strip of pressed, pale dirt leading out of town.

He nodded. "Want to turn around?"

"I don't *want* to . . ." Ellen said tentatively, laughing.

"Neither do I," her father said.

He set his watch back. It took an instant, a twirl of the tiny hands, and they were free. Ellen felt a thrill of mischief. She did not think of her mother, only of a hurdle she and her father had leapt together. As they rode on, she stared greedily at each dry bush and blotched, scampering pig.

"When I was eighteen," her father said, "I bought a motorcycle and rode around Europe for months."

Ellen had never heard this before. "Was it fun?" she asked.

"I lived like a maniac."

She paused, unsure whether this was good or bad. "Was it fun?" she asked again.

"Fun. Was it fun." He stared across the miles of dead grass and shook his head. "It was the best time of my life."

Ellen felt suddenly shy. She followed her father's gaze to the horizon, where faded earth nudged a faded sky. It looked like the edge of something hidden, a place he alone had explored.

"Let's go," she said, kicking the shaggy sides of her pony. As it stamped into the hot, dry wind, she felt a longing never to go back.

"You're a hooligan," her father said, laughing when he'd caught up to her.

"I'm a maniac," Ellen said.

The sun was low when they finally returned to the beach. Ellen's mother, Vivian, waited on the cooling sand. When she saw them, she jumped to her feet. "Thank God!" she cried. "I thought you'd been robbed or something."

"This goddam watch," Ellen's father said. "I swear it's running backward."

"Well, lunch is here if you want it," Ellen's mother said. "Then I guess we'd better pack."

Ellen sank onto the sand and began eating frantically. The sandwiches were warm from hours in the heat. Her mother didn't ask where Ellen and her father had been, she just gazed across the water. It was the last day of their vacation.

"I'm sorry, Mom," Ellen said through a mouthful of food. "I'm sorry you were by yourself."

Her father cleared his throat and stood up.

Her mother looked at Ellen curiously. "Relax," she said, smiling. "What could you have done?"

In the five years since that trip, there had been no time for family vacations. Ellen's father traveled too much on business. This year he was selling franchises for Tommy's, a lobster restaurant in downtown Detroit. "They use real butter—sweet butter," he would tell prospective investors. "Quality like that is a dying art." Ellen imagined sometimes that Tommy was the name of his child from an earlier marriage, some young prodigy living in another state.

At one time Ellen's mother had gone with him on some of his trips. But lately she'd stayed home, conditioning her hair and soaking her Boston ferns in the kitchen sink. She grew thin, and reminisced about their trips.

"I was almost killed in Jamaica," she said at breakfast one day. "Your dad swam away from our boat and a wind came up. I started sailing out to sea." She spoke with the urgency of a first telling, though Ellen had heard the story many times.

"Jesus, what a nightmare," her father said, looking up from his

118

paper. "You were going so fast I couldn't catch up. I was splashing around, screaming how to turn the boat, but you couldn't hear me."

"So what happened?" Ellen cried, caught in the story.

"I jumped off," her mother said. "I swam back to your father. The boat kept going." She was washing apples in the kitchen sink. Now she stopped, still holding the colander under the running faucet, and turned to Ellen's father. They looked at each other, and Ellen felt a current of something between them that startled her.

After a moment they looked away. Her mother shook the colander under the water. Ellen heard apples bumping against its sides. Her father put on his coat, shaking the sleeves gently over his arms. He was leaving for the airport, catching a plane to Australia.

"I have an idea," he said, kissing them each goodbye. "Easter's six weeks away. We'll go back to Puerto Vallarta."

While her father was in Australia, Ellen went with her friend Renata to Mama Santos, a Mexican restaurant in Glencoe. It was a train ride outside Chicago, but Renata's brother, Eric, was a bartender there and had promised to serve them alcohol. Ellen had never been to a bar before. She ordered a rum cocktail crowded with small umbrellas and leaned back, crossing her legs in a way she hoped was sophisticated. Then, at a corner table half hidden by a ficus, Ellen saw her father.

She sat very still, lips on her straw, and tried to make sense out of this. He had left for Australia six days before and was not due back for four more. He sat with another man and two women, one of whom wore the striped tennis sweater Ellen had given her father last Christmas. The woman had on salmon-colored lipstick. Her hand rested on Ellen's father's shoulder.

Ellen carefully set down her glass. She blinked at her smeared reflection in the strip of brass that ran along the bar, then looked back at her father. He had a large dynamic face shaped like the spade on a playing card. His eyes were silvery gray. Ellen was struck by how handsome he looked—handsome the way strangers are, people on buses or in the supermarket. A terrible emptiness opened inside her stomach. Her father was handsome, a handsome man in a restaurant surrounded by other handsome people who were his friends. He talked, he moved his hands, and as Ellen watched she felt that she herself had no right to be here. He belonged wherever he was.

When the group stood up, she swiveled toward the bar and hunched over her drink. Renata had gone to the bathroom, and Eric was washing glasses at the sink. Ellen heard her father's loud laugh right behind her, and was overcome by sudden, dreamlike calm, as if a part of her had shut off, or gone to sleep. A car pulled up to the restaurant. There were shoes on the pavement, laughter, shutting doors. When the left rear door stuck and had to be slammed twice, Ellen knew the car was her father's. Six days before, he'd driven that car to the airport. Ellen had waved goodbye to him through the tinted windshield.

When she heard only silence, Ellen slid from her stool and went outside. She was panting, and her heartbeat made her dizzy. It was dusk. A curved driveway arched toward the door of the restaurant, and beyond it sprawled the wide suburban parking lot. Ellen looked across it. She stared at the passing cars, at the pale moon rising over the asphalt. She felt a pain somewhere inside her but couldn't find its source. "Where does it hurt?" her mother would ask if she were there. "Where does it hurt the most?" It hurt everywhere, Ellen thought. It didn't hurt enough.

She searched the frail rim of trees around the parking lot, the sky soaked with dusk. Two hours before, she and Renata had skipped across this lot, running their hands along Cadillacs and loudly debating what drinks they should have. Martinis? Bloody marys? Piña coladas? It seemed an ancient memory, a scene from her childhood. Ellen longed to pick up where that memory ended, to burrow in the company of Eric and Renata, but this seemed impossible now. He was gone. He'd driven away in his car with the blond woman and his friends, leaving to Ellen this restaurant, this parking lot, this iridescent sky. They looked like nothing.

During the ride back to Chicago, Ellen rocked against the seat of Eric's car, impatient to throw herself in her mother's arms and be soothed. Her mother had long, cool hands and hair like a lioness's. She was the most comforting person on earth.

Ellen found her mother seated on the living room floor, her hair in a scarf. She had the dreamy look she often wore after spending several hours by herself. "I'm rearranging," she said. "Dusting."

Around her lay things she had bought on her various trips: inlaid wood chests, corn-husk dolls, animals carved from ivory. In a glass dish were the colored marble eggs she had bought with Ellen's father in Florence. Ellen felt a nervous fluttering under her ribs.

"I've lost perspective," her mother said. "Can you see any difference?"

Ellen wished she were back at the age when she would howl shamelessly while her mother used a tweezer to pick bits of gravel from her skinned knees. Her mother looked as delicate now as the blown-glass vase she was holding.

"Mom," Ellen said.

Her mother looked up. The room was very still. Ellen felt the weight of the old house, its dense curtains and clean, swept kitchen. Her mother's world was pure, steadfast, decent. But it wasn't enough for him.

"What is it?" her mother asked.

Ellen sank to the floor and lifted a crimson egg from the dish. She felt a ghastly power, the kind she felt sometimes when using a knife or scissors. Once, while chopping celery, she had glanced at her mother's pale arm and thought with horror of how easily she could cut the soft skin. She had pictured the bright stripe of blood, her mother's startled look of pain. She had tortured herself with these thoughts for several moments before putting down the knife and wrapping her mother tightly in her arms. As she hugged, her mother began to laugh. "Such affection," she said. "What have I done to deserve this?"

"Oh, your father called tonight," she said now. "From Sydney. He sends a kiss."

Ellen stared at her. "How's he doing?" she managed to ask.

"Lonely," said her mother. "At least the weather's good."

Ellen leaned back against her hands. She watched the long cords of her mother's neck, the fragile blade of her chin, and was suddenly furious at her for letting herself be fooled, for knowing less than Ellen did. "How come you don't go with him anymore?" Ellen demanded.

Her mother shrugged. "He's busy." She polished another egg, then looked back at Ellen. "What makes you ask?"

Now Ellen felt a surge of guilt, as if she and her father were in this thing together. She avoided her mother's eyes. "I don't know."

"He works too hard," her mother said.

Ellen's father brought her a glass paperweight shaped like a kangaroo and a T-shirt that said SYDNEY. She felt senseless, goofy relief as he talked about the vineyards he had seen, their red dirt and acrid smell of ripeness. The night at Mama Santos was something separate, something cordoned off. It made no difference. She thought about it constantly.

Ellen and her parents flew to Puerto Vallarta two days before Easter. They rented a small house outside of town, where flowers poured from the cliffs in a bright, clotted rush. Their first morning, they sat outside on the terrace, eating sweet Mexican rolls and drinking coffee.

"Remember Ed Morgan?" her father said. "He's building some condos up the hill. I should take a look, the poor bastard."

Her mother rolled her eyes. "Ed Morgan," she said. "I think I'll meet you in town."

Ellen watched her father. She watched him constantly now, searching for signs of restlessness or boredom. Often his eyes had the fractured, glossy look of something repaired with too much glue. He would glance at his watch as though tracking events somewhere else. Ellen felt a continual need to distract him, to hold his attention.

"I'll go with you," she said.

"It's hot up there, squirrel."

"So?"

Her parents exchanged looks of surprise. Ellen felt her mother's gaze, the kind eyes in a face as rigid and spare as a kitchen table. She could still remember a time when her mother would lie in bed on weekends with a cup of cocoa, eating croissants Ellen's father brought from the French bakery. He would rest his head on her stomach and protest that she was dropping crumbs in his eyes. "Oh hush," Ellen's mother would say, licking her fingers one at a time. But she wasn't like that now. She was a person who got left in other people's wakes.

Ellen and her father drove up the mountain road in a rattling

Jeep. His elbow pointed out the window. Ellen pointed her own the same way. She kept her eyes on the wet curl of growth that sprang from the red dirt. Beside them, cliffs dropped straight to the sea.

"Am I like Mom?" she asked.

"In some ways," he said. "Although you've got my adventurous streak—that's a difference." He used one finger to steer the car. When Ellen learned to drive this year, she would drive like that.

"Could get you into trouble," he added, grinning.

Ellen smiled at the wind, letting it dry her lips and teeth. "I hope so," she said.

Ed Morgan had a greasy cream-colored beard and the sort of skin that can grow only more red. He picked his way toward them over mounds of steaming earth. Skeleton houses dotted the land: fresh blond planks shimmering in the midday sun. A bulldozer smeared the air with its heat.

"I didn't know you had a daughter," Ed said, pouring them each a vodka at a flimsy outdoor table.

Ellen's father chuckled. "I keep her hidden."

"No wonder," Ed said, winking at Ellen as he handed her a glass. He gave off a meaty smell, as if the sun had partially cooked him. The heat soaked Ellen's dark hair, making her feel almost faint.

"You may want to skip the booze, squirrel," her father said.

He watched as she lifted her glass. Ellen sensed that he was nervous, and felt a rare, tenuous power over him. She took a large sip. "Delicious," she lied.

Her father smiled uneasily and looked at his watch. "We're in and out of here," he said.

"Relax," Ed told him. "Hang around a little."

He topped off Ellen's glass, filling it so high that the vodka spilled on her fingers when she tried to lift it. She and Ed toasted and drank. Vodka flooded her throat, gagging her. She felt almost frantic, desperate to keep the tiny edge she'd gained on her father, no matter what it took. He watched her, shifting in his seat.

"How go the legal battles?" he asked Ed.

Ed sighed. "About the same. Only the lawyers win."

Ellen took another sip. It brought tears to her eyes.

"Look at this," Ed said, watching Ellen with surprise. "Chip off the old block."

Her father laughed weakly. "Christ, let's hope not."

When it became too hot to sit still, Ed took them on a tour of his construction site. Ellen was barely able to keep her balance as they clambered over the hot, soft earth.

"Take my arm, squirrel," her father said, watching her with concern. Ellen could see he was anxious to get away. She asked every question she could think of to draw out the visit.

Finally they reached the Jeep. Ed's face was scarlet, running with sweat. He looked on the verge of collapse. Ellen felt a sudden great affection for this harmless, clownish man who had been her accomplice. She was sorry to leave him. When the men had shaken hands, she kissed Ed goodbye on the lips.

Her father gripped the wheel with both hands as they headed back down the mountain. "I don't think vodka at noon is such a good idea, squirrel," he said in an easy, joking way. But he wasn't smiling.

"You drank," Ellen said, letting her head loll against the seat. "You drink a lot."

"Your mother's not going to like it."

"Are we telling her?"

He glanced at Ellen, then back at the road. "Well no," he said. "I guess we'd better not."

Ellen watched the ocean awhile, her head spinning. "What are Ed's legal battles?" she asked.

Her father explained that Ed had owned a company in Chicago that went bankrupt three years before. Now he was being sued by his former investors.

"Is he guilty?" Ellen asked.

Her father hesitated. "He lied too much," he said. "If he'd told some truth and let the pressure off, he'd be in a lot less trouble now."

Ellen wondered if this meant he was guilty or not. "What do you mean, 'lied too much'?"

"He should've told just enough to win people over," her father explained. "Enough to look honest."

Ellen nodded in silence.

"As little as possible, but something."

"I see."

"If you have to lie, you're already in danger."

They rode in silence. Shortly before they reached town, Ellen turned to her father, raising her voice above the sound of the engine. "Dad, have you gone out with anyone else since you and Mom were married?" she asked.

His gray eyes were fastened to the road. "Of course not."

"If the answer was yes, would you tell me?"

Her father sighed. "No, squirrel," he said. "I probably wouldn't."

"But then you'd be in danger. Right?"

Her father didn't answer, and Ellen let it drop.

Ellen's mother was not at the café where they had arranged to meet. Her father put his hands in his pockets and stared at the breaking waves, which were crowded with the bobbing heads of children. He looked at his watch. "We're late," he said.

They sat without speaking. Her father ordered a beer and drank it quickly. "Let's take a look around," he said.

The streets were crowded with Mexican families celebrating the holiday. There were women in black dresses made of cotton, girls whose thin, dusty legs teetered over high heels as they trod the mud streets. The air smelled of bitter Mexican beer.

Ellen's father stayed close to her as they wove among the crowds. He would crane his neck to look for her mother, then glance quickly back at Ellen. She began to wander more often from his side, peering with sudden interest into the windows of shops while her father rushed to retrieve her.

Finally he put his arm around her, cupping her shoulder in his palm. His hand was large and warm, and Ellen relaxed in the safety of his grip. She steered him into a sweetshop, where he bought her coffee ice cream on a heat-softened sugar cone. In a silversmith's window a pair of turquoise earrings caught her eye.

"Better wait till we get home before you put these on," her father said, chuckling as he counted out the bills. "They're pretty flashy."

Ellen smiled sweetly and slipped the earrings on.

So much attention from her father was exhausting, and she felt a giddy tremor rising from her stomach. She tossed her head, so that the earrings bumped her cheek. She looked for her mother, hoping not to find her.

Finally they stopped. Her father shielded his eyes and turned in a full circle, staring over the crowds. A group of children scampered past, dragging a blue donkey-shaped piñata through the dust. Young men leaned in doorways and wandered in restless groups. Ellen noticed some of them watching her, and was conscious of her thin, bare arms, the tiny hairs on her thighs.

"I have an idea," her father said. "I'll ask the guy in that shop if he's seen her. It's the kind of place she likes." He pointed to a store that sold clay jugs sprinkled with a thin, clear glaze that looked like sugared water. Beyond it, several men in bare feet and hats lounged against a wall.

"I'll wait out here," Ellen said.

"Come on, squirrel. It'll take a second." He took her elbow, but Ellen pulled away.

"I'll wait," she insisted, flushing to the neck.

Her father's eyes darted along the street. "Just don't move," he said, jogging toward the shop. "I mean it, squirrel. You stay put."

The instant he was gone, Ellen moved closer to the men by the wall. A few shielded their eyes to look up at her. They were squatting in the dust, passing a bottle around. She stood before them with one leg bent, staring at the exhausted plaster between their shoulders. Her heart was beating fast. She glanced back at the shop to make sure her father hadn't reappeared. His Spanish was poor; the conversation would take a while. Her own mischief struck her as irrepressibly funny, and she gritted her teeth to keep from laughing.

They were young men, smooth-faced and a little shy. They spoke to her in Spanish, but Ellen smiled and shrugged her helplessness. They laughed, shaking their heads, and Ellen glimpsed herself through their eyes: a thin girl of sixteen with long strands of dark hair, resisting the flow of traffic to display herself before these men. It was a senseless, hilarious sight. She felt like weeping.

One of the men rose slowly to his feet and came toward her. *"Hola, chica,"* he said.

Ellen smiled at him. She felt as though some force were acting on her, making her breathless and dizzy. *"Hola,"* she said, extending her hand as if she and the man had just been introduced.

He took her hand and held it tightly. When Ellen tried to slide from his grip, he clenched harder, so that it hurt. He was grinning. Ellen felt the pulse of blood through his hand, sweat gathering between his skin and hers. She found herself grinning helplessly back at him, transfixed by the danger. The other men called and clapped, stamping their feet on the dirt. The music seemed louder. The man who was holding her hand adjusted his grip and began to pull her down the street.

Ellen resisted him, barely moving despite the man's violent tugs to her arm. Her mind worked frantically: Why had she done this? What was going on? Being pulled down the street by this stranger seemed the culmination of a wildness that had been in her for weeks, and she recoiled from it now. It sickened her.

Ellen heard running behind her, the sound of her father's shouts. He pushed the man away, knocking him into the dust. The man landed in a roll, and when Ellen's father pursued him, he sprang to his feet, poised in a crouch. He was holding a knife, pointing its long blade straight at Ellen's father's heart. Her father froze. A whimper rose in Ellen's throat, and he turned at the sound. The man with the knife slipped into the throng.

Ellen's father grabbed her and pulled her to him so hard that her head knocked the bones of his chest. She found that she was crying. The sweet tastes of vodka and ice cream hung at the back of her throat, and she gulped them down. Her father stroked her hair. Through his ribs Ellen heard the urgent beating of his heart.

Ellen's mother wandered from an alley. She walked slowly, carrying packages wrapped in paper. Wedged in a cone of newsprint was a bouquet of crepe flowers: dry, colored petals fastened together with wire.

"Vivian!" Ellen's father cried. "Christ, where have you been?"

"You were late," she said, looking rather pleased. "I got sick of waiting."

She kissed the top of Ellen's head, and Ellen relaxed against her mother, relieved that she was back. She felt shaken, full of dread.

"Keeping up with you two is some job," her father said.

"You're out of practice," her mother said.

Ellen's father put an arm around each of them and steered them toward the beach. He held tightly, and it seemed to Ellen that he cared for them more now, at this moment, than he had in a long time. He was scared, that was why. It made her sad.

He led them to a restaurant near the beach. A virulent sun lay close to the horizon, and the air felt steamy and dense. Ellen's father leaned back and clasped his hands behind his head. Then he flattened them on the table and spread the fingers.

"I've got a confession to make," he said. "I've had an affair. One. In eighteen years of marriage."

They stared at him. He was folding and unfolding his napkin. The cloth shook in his fingers. He looked up suddenly, before Ellen could look away, and their eyes locked. "Two years ago," he said, speaking directly at Ellen. "In Kansas City, Missouri. A salesgirl I met on her lunch break."

Ellen looked at her woven place mat and listened to her heart. It bumped in a scary, irregular way, and she wondered if she were old enough to have a heart attack.

Her mother sat up straight. "Why in God's name are you saying this now?" she asked.

He didn't answer. His eyes were still on Ellen. She thought of that day when he'd moved the hands of his watch, her delight at being part of the conspiracy. She looked at him now: handsome, grave, penitent. Following him would be so easy, she'd done it for years. But where would it lead?

"He's lying," she said.

Her mother's lips parted. Light shone along the bottoms of her teeth.

Ellen stood up. "Lying," she said again, letting the word rise from her mouth like a bubble. "He never went to Australia. I saw him in a restaurant with a girl."

Without another word Ellen turned and walked toward the sea, letting the breeze fill her ears and block out every other sound. The water was rough, and its frothy edges bubbled over her feet. Ellen took a few more steps until the churning water scrubbed her shins, then her thighs. She had an urge to swim in her clothes, to feel the fabrics float around her in the warm tide.

Slowly she moved forward, letting the water cover her by degrees. Then a wave reared in front of her, and Ellen dove into it. There was a hard, salty blow to her head, and she was beyond the breaking surf.

Several minutes later she saw her mother on the beach. Ellen called to her and waved her arms, expecting to be ordered ashore immediately. Instead, her mother moved closer to the water, keeping her eyes on Ellen. She stepped into the waves with great care, as if fearful of sharp things hidden in the sand. Soon the rim of her dress floated around her waist. Standing that way, she looked like a girl, and Ellen was struck by the thought that her mother had once been her own age. She saw this now in the fine pale bones of her face, the wet hair sticking to her head.

"Swim," Ellen called to her.

Her mother hesitated, then pushed off. She swam in the smooth, even crawl she used for laps in a pool. The waves jostled her, upsetting the neat strokes.

When she finally reached Ellen, her eyebrows were raised in a look of prolonged amazement. Her head seemed small in its slick coating of hair. "We've lost our minds," she said with a high, nervous laugh.

Ellen was aware of not thinking about her father, and this gave her a tenuous sense of freedom. Her mother treaded water, looking up at the sky. Suddenly she turned to Ellen and grasped her hand underwater. Ellen felt her mother grow perfectly still. After a moment she let go of Ellen's hand and began swimming back. Ellen followed.

A wave washed them in, and Ellen found herself sprawled beside her mother on the sand. Her father was nowhere in sight. Her mother's frail limbs showed through her wet dress. Ellen looked down at her own Mexican shirt and saw that its bright pinks and greens had drained away. A sudden despair overwhelmed her. She buried her feet in the sand and grasped a damp, gritty handful in each fist. She had an urge to put some in her mouth and suck the coarse grains.

"What's going to happen?" she asked, ashamed of the tremor in her voice.

Her mother was kneeling, shivering a little. She put an arm around Ellen's shoulders. "We're going back to the house to dry off," she said. "That's what."

She pulled her daughter to her feet, surprising Ellen with the strength of her arms. Ellen leaned against her mother, allowing herself to be led through the sand. The sun had dropped below the horizon.

"And then we're getting out of this," her mother said.

SPANISH WINTER

I've been an off-season traveler since my divorce, and this winter I'm in Spain. A man is following me. On the train from Madrid he was a copper salesman with an eager mustache and samples of his product: copper wires, copper disks, copper beaten into thin, pliable sheets. I took everything he gave me and stuffed it into my purse. In Córdoba he was a restaurant owner who fed me plate after plate of sizzling beef while I watched the rain slide from the awning of his restaurant. I ate until my face began to throb. Sweat gathered on my upper lip.

"The senorita is very hungry," the man said, filling my glass with red wine. "The senorita has been underfed."

I nodded, too full to struggle with my college Spanish.

The truth is, I'll take anything I'm given.

———

In Toledo, where I have just been, the man was tall and gaunt as an ascetic. He wore a white turtleneck and was feeding squares of marzipan to children in the central square. It was nearly midnight. The air blurred with fog that rose from the surrounding river. The bare trees were strung with small white lights.

I sat on a bench and waited. When the children had gone, the man came and sat beside me. He had a wretched face, gaunt and beaten and sad. "You are alone?" he said in Spanish.

"Is there any more candy?" I asked.

He handed me a piece wrapped in translucent colored plastic. It was the softest marzipan, the kind Toledo is famous for. I ate with tiny bites to make it last, letting each piece melt between my tongue and teeth. I knew what was coming, but did not look forward to it.

The man's eyes never left me: the frank, sad eyes that clowns have. When I finished he stood and reached for my hand. I followed him out of the square and down a tiny side street.

His house was near the cathedral. It was stately, decayed, owned by his family for centuries. An El Greco hung in the entry, a portrait of some dead relation. I thought at first it was him.

"Toledo was El Greco's home, do you know?"

I shook my head, although of course I did.

"Ay!" he cried. "Toledo is famous for this. Here is where you must go tomorrow . . ."

I settled back in a velvet chair and let him teach. I like advice, even when I don't need it.

"Why come to Spain for this season?" he asked. "Even the Spaniards want to escape."

"The museums aren't crowded," I joked.

"You are lonely. I can see in your face."

"I'm waiting for something to happen."

He leaned forward, gazing at the red velvet folds surrounding his four-poster bed. A carved procession of fat knights on horseback marched down and around each post toward the satin sheets. "Is there a difference?" he asked.

One cool, skeletal hand reached for my knee.

Early the next day I took the train to Granada.

Spain in wintertime is dangerous and beautiful and empty. I wander alone through the embroidered stone of the Alhambra, columns and honeycomb, a weave of colored tiles that makes me dizzy. A man sells peanuts baked in sugar, gravelly and sweet. I buy a bag. I sit on a bench and close my eyes and let the winter sun pour across my face.

I'm thirty-two years old. In my thirty-two years I've gone to college, married, and had a daughter whose hair is pale and soft as the grain of fresh-cut wood. Her name is Penny, and she chooses to live with her father.

I met my husband on a beach in Mexico, where I'd gone with some girls from my sorority right after college. I can see myself exactly as I was: a tall, knock-kneed girl gathering abalone shells in the skirt of her dress.

"Have you been to the tide pools yet?" my future husband asked me.

He was older than any boys I'd known in college. I followed him over a low rocky promontory that reached into the breaking waves. The rocks were sharp, and we moved slowly. I kept my eyes on the spectacle at my feet: shallow pools filled with sea urchins and small crabs, bright anemones that flung open their soft tentacles at

each burst of seawater. There were endless, glistening shards of abalone.

"I can't believe this!" I cried.

I dropped to my knees and began scooping up the treasures. My future husband stood above me, smiling down. Then he knelt on a rock and helped me pry an urchin from its hiding place. Soon he was venturing farther into the surf, taken with the adventure of it.

"Look at this!" he shouted, waving an orange starfish. "This one just about killed me."

I loaded up his pockets, soaking his khaki pants. My sundress was a wide basket for dripping sea creatures. Walking back, feeling the warm, wet breeze on my bare legs, I knew he was watching me. At each rough part, he gripped my shoulders. I began teetering on purpose. He was thirty-five, I almost twenty-one, when we married.

As I descend the path from the Alhambra, two boys leap at me from among the trees. They are tall and skinny, with sharp, beardless chins. One of them holds a switchblade. "Give us everything," he says.

I hand him my wallet.

"All of it," the other hisses.

"There's nothing else."

The knife flashes. The boy cuts the strap of my purse and begins opening its zippered pockets. I picture my toothbrush, a powder puff, the bits of copper the man on the train gave me. They are precious, meaningless things, and I want them back.

"There's nothing valuable in there," I tell him.

In a single flicker of movement, the empty-handed boy snatches the gold chain from my neck. It's real gold, a gift from my husband. The boy pulls hard, leaving a thin burn along my skin. They run away, skidding on the dry leaves. I watch my purse weave among the tree trunks and out of sight.

As I plod back, I am filled with a dismal triumph. I feel relief, the relief of being one step closer to something inevitable. The pleasure of ceasing to resist, of giving up.

I wander through Granada's crowded streets. My bag is still at the hotel, but I don't go back yet. The air smells of sugar-baked loaves the vendors are selling from carts. It's nine-thirty, nearly dinnertime. Children run and call, scrambling down narrow lanes toward the central square. I follow. In the middle of the square a man sells colorful balloon-animals attached to long sticks. The children who surround him draw back at my approach.

"I've been robbed," I tell the man.

His face is creased and bare, like cloth that has been folded a long time and then laid flat. He packs his balloons in a leather case. Children whisper to each other with thin, silver voices. Lamps hang from the trees, and I follow the man through their patches of light. I feel myself begin to smile, trusting and alert, following a man I have followed all my life.

When my husband told me he was leaving, we were sitting in our den. I looked around at the polished shelves, the TV and VCR, piles of *The New Yorker* and *Business Week*. The accumulation of ten years of marriage, mostly his.

"I've made the arrangements," he told me. "I'll rent an apartment."

I ran my eyes along his encyclopedias, photos he'd taken of whitewashed churches in Greece, a crusty turquoise horse from some ancient dynasty. "All this is yours," I said.

"We can settle that when the time comes . . ."

"You stay here," I told him. "I'll go."

This took him by surprise. "Do you want that?"

A terrible feeling had taken hold of me. I searched the room for things of my own and found nothing but things my husband had given me: a kimono pinned to the wall, *The Complete Works of Shakespeare,* a set of Greek worry beads.

"What have I got to lose?" I said.

He sighed. "Don't be a martyr."

I grabbed the bottle of wine we were sharing and threw it against a wall. There was a sumptuous crash and red wine splashed across an Indian rug he'd bought in Arizona. My husband leaned back in his seat and gazed up at me. "You're a child," he said.

Now, when I think of his new wife making eggs for my daughter in what used to be my kitchen, I feel a pleasant ache. The grim satisfaction of a clean sweep.

It takes three days to straighten things out: passport, traveler's checks, hours at the police station waiting my turn to explain the simple crime. All of this annoys me. When a thing is gone it's gone, is what I think. Soon there will be nothing left, and in a sense I look forward to this, although it frightens me.

I spend these days of waiting in cafés, writing postcards to Penny. At home she will attach them to the refrigerator using fruit-shaped magnets. She does this carefully, plotting my journey in perfect sequence. When I return she will narrate it like a story.

When Penny lived with me, I brought her something every day: Magic Markers, hair ribbons, candy. I tortured myself, convinced she needed more, that nothing I bought or said or did could satisfy her.

"There's a hole in our lives, is that what you're thinking?" I demanded last winter as we sat alone in the vast dining room of a beach resort, the sound of rain mingling with the breaking surf. We were the only guests at the hotel.

Penny surveyed the white tablecloth. "Where's a hole?" she said.

"You're thinking none of this is right, aren't you? That it's all just slightly off?"

She gazed at me with her wide brown eyes, trying to see what answer I wanted. "I don't know," she said timidly.

"I don't blame you for feeling like that," I said, rising from my chair and pacing before the window. "I feel it, too."

Penny stopped eating and stared into her bowl, where pale cereal floated.

"Now I've made you sad," I cried, dancing around her. "There, sit up straight and forget what I said. Eat."

Miserably, she held the spoon in her fist. She glanced at my abandoned plate of eggs. "You eat, too," she said.

We sat in silence. Her lip began to quiver.

I loomed over her. "What?" I said. "Say what you're thinking!"

"I miss Daddy."

They were the words I most dreaded, yet I felt relief. I sank back in my chair and lifted her into my lap. Through the web of her ribs I felt her heart beating rapidly. Two pigtails sat pertly on her head. I kissed the white arc of her part and breathed its sweet, oatmeal scent.

"I'll take you back," I said. "We'll leave today."

She was the last to go, the hardest to part with.

Nights I spend with the man who sells balloon-toys. He lives on the outskirts of town in a tiny high-rise apartment with a balcony he is very proud of. He takes me out there to appreciate the view, which is mostly of TV antennas. We hardly speak. (My Spanish isn't good.)

His room smells of those small green olives that taste so excellent with wine. If he has any, though, he doesn't share them with me.

Mornings, he sits on his balcony wrapped in a coat and smokes thin brown cigarettes. I lie in bed, looking up at the ceiling fan and trying to remember my life before I married. I know I must have had one: long, easy days studying the works of Botticelli, sprawled on the college green with my friends. But I glimpse these scenes like pictures, never from inside. It could be another person's life.

After smoking for an hour or so, the balloon man climbs back into bed with me. He's a skinny Spaniard with a sudden, crooked smile. In another life I might have loved this man, even married him. As it is, I lie beneath him and stare up at the fan, its long blades immobile in winter.

Finally the passport chores are done. I spread my map across a café table, as my husband used to do. I consider my options.

"Alison?" a man says.

I can't place him. He has that elfin sort of face which doesn't age, pale eyes, and strong square hands.

"Rutgers," he says. "Remember?"

I do, then. He was not a friend exactly, more one of those people I had known about and spoken to occasionally. "John?"

"Jake."

"Weren't you always selling something? You had a lot of business schemes?"

"Bravo." He eases into a chair beside me. I remember now that he ran a business typing students' papers. Later he sold shares in a card-counting venture in Atlantic City. He had seemed so much a man of the world that just sitting beside him made you feel nostalgic, as though he were already beyond those college years, looking back, and you were one of his memories.

"So, what have you been doing?" I ask. "How many companies have you chaired?"

"This and that." He taps the table's edge as if testing for hidden compartments. "Nothing earthshaking."

"That's hard to believe."

"And you?"

I take a deep breath, and only then does it strike me what a terrible process I've initiated. My life teeters before me like a bad view from an unsteady height. "It's a long story," I say, feeling my smile wane. "Not worth it."

"Ditto." He takes off his glasses, which are shaded beige, and rubs the skin between his eyes. The lids are pink at the edges. I have an odd sense that we have just exchanged a confidence.

"You, ah . . . waiting for your husband or something?"

"Right," I say, pleased by this suggestion. "He's at the Alhambra. I wasn't up to the climb today."

"I hear you. My wife's up there, too."

"How funny!" I cry, unable to resist. "I wonder if they'll meet."

I feel lighthearted, as if nothing had happened to me yet. I imagine myself standing in a cafeteria line, holding a blue plastic tray. In my mind, it is late spring, and the grass is green and fat.

"Do you know, I was robbed up there the other day?" I tell Jake. "Two boys got everything. My passport . . . I had to buy this bag."

I hold it up. It's made of the softest calfskin, that fine leather for which Spain is famous. For two days I have held it in my lap, smelling the sweet new leather each time I breathe. At night I leave it open beside the balloon man's bed so I can smell it as I go to sleep.

He feels the seams. "It's good quality," he says. "A lot of times they aren't. Where'd you get it?"

"Right nearby. I can show you."

"But your husband . . ."

"Oh, he just left. He'll be gone awhile."

The sunlight in Granada is more pure and strong than any I have felt in Spain this winter. It warms my neck. The soft leather of my new bag rubs pleasantly against my shoulder. I feel the happiness that comes of believing your own lies for a minute. I picture my husband wandering through the halls of the Alhambra, loaded with his guidebooks and maps, describing everything to me at dinner over a bottle of wine.

"You must have a hundred companies by now," I say in a voice I don't quite recognize.

"Not exactly."

"Well, lots then."

"Sure," he says, shrugging. "A few."

"Are some of them in Spain?"

He glances at the sky. "No. None here."

We're near the cathedral. It is very quiet on these backstreets, and their narrowness keeps the sun from touching the pavement. When I find the small corner shop where I bought my leather purse, its gates are down. "Siesta," I say. "Damn."

We stand awkwardly, unsure what to do next. Twice Jake turns to look behind him. "Are you being followed?" I joke.

"No," he says. "Why, are you?"

I adjust my calfskin strap. "Of course not."

"You know," he says. "Seeing you makes me remember my very young self. It's a funny feeling."

"What do you remember?"

"How completely without fear I was."

"Isn't everyone, at that age?"

"Me especially. Too much."

"Now you scare more easily?"

He moves away, hands in his pockets. There is no sound but the squeaking of small black birds that circle overhead. They sound like mice, only more plaintive.

Jake turns to me quickly. "I did a stupid thing," he says. "I've lost a lot of people's money." The skin is white around his mouth.

"How awful."

"It is awful." He breathes as if we had just been running. "I don't know why I told you that."

"It's all right," I say, rubbing my damp palms along the sides of my dress. I want to get away from him.

"Forget I said that."

"Fine."

He pushes his hands inside his pockets and looks at the sky. It is very blue above us.

"I've ruined families, that's what I'm saying. These people have nothing left. Can you imagine what that's like?"

"For you or for them?"

"For them," he says, startled. "Them. Of course."

I run my fingers over the soft leather strap of my purse. I love this purse much better than the first.

"You know what's worse? I cheated them. Set it up that way. Then it went more wrong than I meant."

He is watching the church facade, its broad doors and bulges of plaster. I wonder if I should simply walk away.

"Look at this," he says, laughing abruptly. "They're chasing me around the globe, and here I am in a churchyard spilling my guts to a total stranger."

"We went to college together."

"That's true."

I hold the bag in my arms, hugging the leather to my chest. I watch him pace across the stones.

"I'm leaving Spain today. Going to Morocco, down into Africa. That's a secret," he adds, laughing again. It is a strange, nervous laugh I'm not fond of. He moves close to me. His breath is oddly sweet, and his hands shake. I'm afraid he might faint, and then what will I do with him?

"You know the worst thing? The worst thing is I can't do anything. It's gone. *Finito,* my whole life."

"But you're so young," I say, surprising myself. "How on earth can you say that?"

It's true. He is a young man, frightened as a boy. He grows embarrassed, and his eyes veer down to the shiny stones at our feet. "Christ," he says, shaking his head. "Look, I'm sorry to put you through this. Your husband's probably looking for you . . ."

His whole face trembles. He watches me with a look I recognize: the look I'm sure I must have myself when I watch the normal people living happy lives.

"I don't have a husband," I say, holding his gaze. I feel it coming now: a giddy rush of confession, urgent as nausea. "I have nothing in the world."

Jake is speechless. He stares at me, his mouth open a little, his head tilted to one side. I feel an uneasy desire to move closer to him.

"Are you serious?"

I nod in silence and look away.

The sound of a motor distracts us. Turning, I see two men in puffy jackets on a Vespa. It hurtles down a side street, heading straight for us. I barely have time to look at Jake before the bike ploughs between us at top speed and someone knocks me onto the pavement. I sit up, stunned, rubbing my hip, and see my new calf-skin bag swinging from a motorcyclist's shoulder. I scream at the top of my lungs, and the sound echoes back across the courtyard. The Vespa rounds a corner and disappears.

Jake runs after them, his footsteps following the motor into silence. I stand alone beneath the whirl of squeaking birds and wait. After a while I sit on the church steps and stare at the hem of my dress, bright green against the stone. Minutes pass, too many to continue waiting, but I feel no urge to move. Night is hours away. A man comes and opens the gates to the leather shop. Beautiful bags like mine hang in the windows. I wonder, if I explain to him what happened, whether he might give me another one for free.

On a warm island whose name I can't remember, my husband and his wife have taken Penny on vacation. I imagine the sweet smell the air must have. Pineapple, is it? Flowers? I recall the sticky buds that sprout from the stalks of tough, sappy plants. I can feel their texture as though I were holding one now.

In the churchyard, there are mostly shadows, though sunlight still grazes the tile roofs. I imagine Jake packing his things for Morocco. Was he actually working with the thieves, I wonder, or did he merely see an exit and take it? Anyway, it doesn't matter. He's gone, my possessions are gone, and I am one step nearer a point I've been longing for, it seems: the point of giving up. Yet my mind keeps drifting to Jake—his panicked belief that his life is over—and this seems so sweet, so melodramatic. He's thirty-two, for God's sake. And it strikes me, then, that I'm no older than he is.

Just then he totters from a side street. There is a long tear down one trouser leg, and his shirttails flap in the breeze. He smiles the way I remember him smiling in college, a big sly grin like cartoon foxes have. He raises my leather bag toward the sky. "Nailed the bastards," he pants, handing it to me with care. "Haven't run like that since track."

I pull back the zipper and see my things: familiar, insignificant. I stare at the jumble of shapes and feel my eyes grow wet. "You saved it," I tell him.

Jake's face is red. He clenches and unclenches his fists, running his hands through his hair. He looks at me several times without speaking. "Ever been to Morocco?" he finally asks.

I imagine beaches, crowded cafés, that smell of tanning lotion. From what seems a great distance, these summer things come wafting back. I look around me. Blue shadows sprawl across the stones, and dusk thickens and chills the air. A last stop, I think, before I go back home to begin again. I'm young, headed to Morocco on vacation. In Morocco it is summertime.

LETTER TO
JOSEPHINE

Parker has dragged his lounge chair into the sea, and water washes over his knees and belly. He holds *The History of the Crimean War* above the splashing. The sun burns overhead.

Lucy has never understood how he can read in the sun this way. Especially that sort of book: heavy, hardbound, dull. When he finishes he will begin another instantly. He has brought a dozen books on their vacation, and the Crimean War is the subject of each.

Lucy sits beneath a palm tree, so that the sun touches her fair skin only in small patches. There was a time when she would not let any sun touch her at all, for her white skin became mottled with freckles and she thought they made her look cheap. But as she grows older she doesn't mind the freckles so much, and the sun feels good in small doses.

Lucy sits with a magazine in her lap and watches people. She has only recently begun to know the pleasure of watching others. For many years she could only worry that she herself was being watched, and would hide beneath wide hats and sunglasses and lipstick to avoid people's stares. But lately she has grown more curious, less self-conscious.

The island of Bora Bora attracts a diverse crowd. This is the best hotel on Bora Bora, many say in all of the islands around Tahiti. It is certainly very expensive, though Lucy does not know how expensive, exactly, because Parker handles that. On the beach there are tanned men in their late forties with hairy stomachs and thin gold chains around their necks. Their companions tend to be much younger women with exercise-hardened bodies and light blond streaks in their hair. There are families, too: docile fair-haired children; teenagers who still lie splayed on their deck chairs at high noon like creatures stranded by the receding tide.

A young woman with long blond hair follows her luggage to a bungalow on stilts above the water at the far end of the beach. The bungalows over the water are the very best at the hotel; Lucy and Parker are staying in one as well. The woman wears a Polynesian dress and a flower in her hair. She and the bellboy enter the bungalow, where the bellboy will explain about towels and meals and the woman will marvel at the vivid red flowers that have been tucked into the room's every crevice. She will breathe deeply to savor their perfume. This is what Lucy did when she and Parker arrived eight days before.

The sun is growing quite hot, and Lucy shifts her chair farther into the shade of the palm. She looks forward to lunchtime, when she and Parker will sit in the cool dining room and eat crab salads as they watch the sea. So far, Parker shows no signs of moving. The water splashes gently over his soft belly. He turns another page.

Glancing back down the beach, Lucy spots the blond woman whom she just saw arriving. Now the woman is standing on the deck of her bungalow, wearing a bikini and looking down at the water, which laps at the bungalow's stilts. Lucy watches her climb onto the railing that surrounds the deck and then dive into the sea in a perfect arc. There is hardly a splash. Lucy stares at the spot where the woman disappeared and waits for her to surface. It seems to take a long time, and she reappears some distance from where she landed. Lucy has not seen anyone else dive off the railing of a bungalow that way. It looks very daring—the sort of thing she imagines doing herself, but would never try.

The woman swims parallel with the beach, then emerges from the water not far from where Parker is sitting. She has the delicate slenderness of the very young, a smooth stomach, and long, narrow legs. Her skin is a rich, even brown. She wears a sparkling turquoise bikini, cut high above her hips to emphasize the fluid curve of her waist. The top wraps her tightly. Lucy glances around the beach and sees that many people have noticed the woman; even Parker has looked up from his book. The blonde turns and begins walking back toward her bungalow. Lucy watches her, noting the slim ankles, the golden tint of her skin against the white sand.

"Did you see her?" she says to Parker when finally he joins her under the palm tree.

"Who?" he asks, carefully shaking sand from his book before replacing it in the beach bag.

"The girl!"

He looks at her without expression.

"The one in the water. That beauty. You must have seen."

"Oh, right," he says, rubbing sand from his ankles. "Pretty."

"But did you really look at her? She was perfect! I've never seen anything like it!"

Parker stands up and looks at Lucy. "I said. Pretty."

For some reason Lucy is excited. She wants to talk about this girl. They walk toward the dining room in their beach shifts, Parker carrying his leather sandals in one hand.

"There was something about her. I think she's a movie star or a model or something."

"Really?"

"You just *are* when you look like that. She's probably someone famous we just aren't recognizing."

"It's possible. We missed Gerald Ford on the golf course in Palm Springs, remember that?" he says.

"I wonder why she's here. I wonder if she's making a film or something. I wonder if she's alone."

"I doubt it." Parker snickers.

They have reached the dining room, and the Polynesian hostess seats them at their usual table. Lucy suppresses her urge to talk even more about the woman. She can see Parker isn't interested.

"How's the war coming?" she asks, patting his hand, which is very brown against her own.

"Not bad, not bad. Russia's having a hard time, but its her own fault."

"Well, make sure things work out for the best," she says, giving him a wink.

It is their joke that Parker presides over whichever war he studies. It seems to Lucy that he has read exhaustively on every war that has ever taken place: the Korean, the World Wars, the War of 1812, the American and French Revolutions, Vietnam. She knows nothing about wars and doesn't really care to, but she always tries to sound interested. Parker is careful to tell her just enough.

As they wait for their salads, Lucy looks out over the terrace. The water is a very pale blue. The shore curls gently, a smooth strip of white sand and shifting palm leaves. She sighs. "Beautiful, isn't it?"

Parker looks up. He has been studying the menu, though they have already ordered their usual meal. "We should try the mahimahi sometime," he says. "What did you say?"

"The view . . ."

It is a hot, lazy day. They are becoming torpid from so many days of lying in the sun. They will be ready to go back to Chicago tomorrow.

"It reminds me of that place in France two years ago," Lucy says. "What was that hotel?"

"Can't remember," Parker says. "Never can remember that stuff."

They have been all over the world, Lucy thinks, watching the sea. Yet so little of it has stuck with her. She clings to names, to snapshots and matchbooks, but the many seasons have mingled hopelessly. She used to arrange their photographs according to which bathing suit she was wearing—the polka-dotted one in Cannes, the striped red in Spain. But the sand and water around the bathing suits all look the same.

Full from lunch and wobbling in the heat, they make their way back down the beach. Parker walks slightly ahead, and Lucy can see he is anxious to return to his war. She wonders what to do with her afternoon. She is tired of magazines, tired of swimming over that strangely colored coral she is afraid to step on.

About ten paces from her chair Lucy stops and shields her eyes. The blond woman she saw before lunch is walking along the beach, holding hands with a man. They swing their arms. Lucy lowers herself into her chair without taking her eyes from them.

As they come closer, Lucy sees that the man wears a camera

around his neck. He stops suddenly and takes a step away from the woman, raising the camera to his eyes and looking at her through the lens. At first she pretends to cower, then swipes at his shin with a brown foot. Lucy hears the shutter clicking. The woman stops protesting and smiles, raising one arm to lift the hair away from her face and neck. She rests a hand on her hip, shifting her weight. She is laughing. The man pulls her onto the sand and kisses her until she wriggles away and runs into the sea. He follows.

Lucy forces herself to look away, but after several moments she finds herself watching the swimming couple again. She watches almost without seeing them, her thoughts meandering in the heat.

She thinks of her best friend, Josephine, whom she hasn't seen in many years. She remembers a night when she and Josephine sat on the back porch of Lucy's house, laughing and gossiping into the darkness. A train approached along the nearby tracks, and they were silent as the long chain of cars gashed past. When the last sounds had faded, Lucy took a breath and said, "Parker asked me to marry him."

Josephine had elastic features that could twist and bend into more drastic expressions than most people's. Her mouth popped open. "My God!" she said, and Lucy sighed with relief at the crooked smile and flash of white teeth.

Neither of them said anything for a moment, and then Josephine's low, mischievous giggle filled the night. "You'll be so rich!" She laughed softly.

"Josephine!" It sounded cheap to hear her say it.

"But come on," Josephine said, seeming puzzled by Lucy's hesitation. "The guy's a millionaire."

"I know, but . . ."

"Well, *admit* it, for God's sake."

There was an awkward pause. Lucy felt she must say something, that it must be the right thing.

"Will you help me pull it off?" she timidly asked, and they laughed together at that.

The following weekend, Josephine dragged Lucy from one shopping mall to the next, buying bathing suits for her honeymoon. Josephine brought a tattered *Glamour* along, and would haul it out everywhere they went, pointing to some photo of a pouting girl in a spandex and asking the salesperson, "Have you got this one?"

In the dressing room Lucy would blush at the sight of her pale, skinny figure in the mirror. But Josephine would say, "Fantastic, couldn't be better!" and add yet another suit to the pile. Occasionally Lucy would glance at Josephine's own figure behind her in the mirror, her full breasts and curved hips, and think that Josephine would look far better in these bathing suits than she herself did. Later, writing to Josephine from Barbados, Lucy could not bring herself to admit that she'd been too timid to wear any of the suits they had selected. In the hotel lobby boutique she had purchased a simple one-piece, navy blue. "Sensible," Parker said, and Lucy felt a flash of joy, of relief, standing in the soaring white lobby with her new husband. He was perfect.

Lucy decides she will spend the afternoon writing Josephine a letter. It has been six years since they have spoken, and Lucy rarely thinks of her friend anymore. Yet every now and then she will pause and for an instant will remember Josephine exactly, her bawdy laugh and tangled hair, her passion for magazines. When she thinks of Josephine, Lucy will look around her, at the gleaming piano and shelves of glass figurines if she is in her living room, at the polished floor, and for an instant she will wonder if she is in somebody else's house.

Lucy feels a shadow overhead and looks up. She is still staring at the water, but no one is swimming anymore. Parker looms overhead with his book.

"Finished already?" she asks.

"You bet," he says, rustling through the beach bag. "Whizzed through that one."

"Interesting?" Lucy asks. It isn't often that Parker looks so excited over one of his books.

"I've got lots of ideas about this," he says. "I don't agree with any of these guys, none I've read so far."

"Is that good?"

"It's good if I can come up with an argument of my own and prove it," Parker says. "We'll see." He has fished a pad of paper from the beach bag and holds it against the trunk of the palm tree, scribbling notes.

"So what will you do?"

"Keep reading," he says, preoccupied. He snaps the pad shut and wedges it into the top of his bathing suit, so that it makes a depression in his stomach. Lucy reaches up and pats him there.

Parker returns to their bungalow to get another book. Lucy wonders if he was always so animated at Yale, where as a young man he'd begun a Ph.D. in history. His father, who was grooming Parker to take over the family business, had been apoplectic. Apparently the vision of a massive pharmaceutical company looming at his elbow added just the right frisson to Parker's endeavor, and from what Lucy has gathered, his two years at Yale were deliriously happy. He still talks about it sometimes, usually after a few drinks, hashing out his ideas for dissertation topics and reminiscing about the late-night arguments over Macaulay and Gibbon and Michelet. He has never explained why he quit with only a master's, but it is obvious. Parker is a man of creature comforts. He grew up rich, and it is hard to imagine him living any other way.

Because Parker has taken the writing pad, Lucy cannot begin her letter to Josephine. She hoists herself from her chair and stands in the sun for a moment, wavering from the exertion of standing suddenly in the heat. She stumbles to the edge of the sea and wades in, savoring the relief of the cool water as it climbs her body in stages. Then she plunges in and surfaces, staying close to shore to avoid the frightening waves.

The blond woman and the dark-haired man are lying on the sand. From the water Lucy watches them stand up slowly, like sleepwalkers. The man picks up their towels, and the woman begins collecting their beach things. She leans down straight-legged, so limber she does not have to bend her knees. Maybe she's a dancer, Lucy thinks.

The two begin to wander toward their bungalow, stumbling a little in the heat. The woman puts her hand on the man's neck and pulls him toward her. They stop walking and kiss. When they move again, the woman's fingers are hooked in his swimming trunks. They walk quickly now, despite the heat.

Lucy has been treading water. Now she notices that the current is wafting her gently down the beach toward the bungalows on stilts above the water. She drifts parallel with the walking couple, all the while telling herself she should begin swimming the other way. The man and woman have reached the door to their bungalow and are wiping sand from their bodies and hanging up their towels. He runs his hand over her stomach. Lucy knows she should swim back. The man draws the woman to him and opens the bungalow door with his other hand. Lucy cannot make herself swim away.

She has floated behind their bungalow now, and can see its

sliding glass door through the railing that surrounds its back deck. It is too shadowy for her to see inside the room, but she thinks she can make out two figures there. She hovers, treading water. The current continues to move her, so that she is almost beyond this bungalow and on to the next. Her own is only yards away, and Parker will be reading on the deck. Lucy paddles against the current now, her eyes fixed on the glass door, trying to make out the shapes in the room.

The curtain opens. Lucy sees the blond woman standing in the doorway, her bare breasts vividly white against her tan. She leans there for just a moment, looking over Lucy's head toward the horizon. Lucy freezes, bobbing in the water, praying the woman will not see her. Her gaze hovers on the white breasts and the slim flare of waist. Then, with a flash of brown arms, the curtain shuts and Lucy is alone again.

She paddles numbly toward shore and heaves herself onto the sand. She weaves among sunbathers and collapses into her chair. She tries to catch her breath. Her heart is thumping. The beach is very quiet, nothing moves. The palm rustles softly.

A strange, anticipatory thrill flickers up and down Lucy's spine. She watches the couple's bungalow and thinks of how, right now, in the middle of the day, the two of them are making love. To distract herself, she opens a magazine, but cannot keep from trying to imagine them. She wishes she herself adored lovemaking as she knows some people do, wishes she were daring, risqué, all the things she has never been and will never be.

For a long time Lucy had believed that money came between herself and Josephine—that her friend couldn't stand her being rich. But it wasn't that. Whatever it was began one afternoon a year after she and Parker were married. Lucy was in town visiting her parents, and she and Josephine met at the same Howard Johnson's where they used to go for banana splits as kids. Rain poured down the plate-glass window beside the table where Lucy waited. She remembers hugging Josephine and smelling freshness and rain, seeing her vivid face grow frantic with delight.

"I want to know everything," Josephine began. She took an enormous bite of hamburger, her lipstick smearing the bun. "I can't tell a thing from your letters."

Lucy laughed. "I don't know where to start."

"Anywhere. You pick. Europe, Africa . . ." She grinned over her Coke. "I've started a stamp collection."

Lucy felt shy suddenly. "Well, a lot of the trips are business."

"Do you fly first class?"

The question made Lucy uncomfortable, it was so overt. She gave a brief nod.

"So, is it like we imagined, like in the magazines?" Josephine said. "I mean, you know, do you feel like one of those girls in *Vogue*?"

Lucy squirmed, looking down at her tuna sandwich. "I'm not sure what you mean."

Josephine's eyes narrowed. She took another bite. There was an uncomfortable silence.

"Tell what you've been up to," Lucy said.

Josephine had a boyfriend who sold sports equipment. She was taking painting classes at the Y. Lucy relaxed while her friend did the talking, but too soon the description ended.

"What does it look like from an airplane, when you land at night?" Josephine asked. "I always try to imagine it, how cities must look from above with all their lights blinking. Is it pretty?"

Lucy pictured herself and Parker in an airplane, both of them tired and eager to land. "Well, it's . . ." she paused, wondering what Josephine wanted her to say. She longed to say the right thing, to acknowledge the beauty without dwelling on it in a way that would seem self-satisfied. "It is pretty," she said. "But you get used to it."

Sure enough, Josephine looked disappointed. "You're not eating your sandwich," she said. Then she leaned across the table and took Lucy's hand in her strong, warm grip. "Is Parker treating you right?" she asked, looking directly into Lucy's face.

Lucy drew back a little. "Sure," she said. "What makes you ask?"

"You seem"—Josephine cocked her head—"I don't know, different. I just wondered."

Lucy hesitated. The problem was that she wasn't used to talking about airplane lights and riding first class. With Parker she simply did them. Being with Josephine demanded another side of herself, the side that used to pore over magazines and imagine living other people's lives. Parker was practical; he would never understand that sort of thinking. She had fallen out of the habit.

Josephine's apple pie arrived, and she heaped a bite with ice cream and ate vigorously. Her jaws flexed under her wide cheekbones. "You remember," she began, speaking slowly, "how we used to imagine being rich? Do you remember that?"

Lucy nodded. She sensed from Josephine's tone that this was a last attempt to get at some basic thing. "Yes . . ." she said, cautiously.

"All I'm asking is, is it actually like that?"

Lucy considered. It was true, there had been moments when she'd thought, I can't believe this is happening to me. The feeling came sometimes when she and Parker traveled, sometimes just when she looked around her own house at the fireplace and thick rugs, at the vast green lawn outside. Whenever she had that feeling, Lucy longed to tell someone. She would turn to Parker, who was usually reading, or anyone else who was there, but no one ever behaved as if anything special were happening. Soon her wonderment would begin to fade. As time went on, it came less and less often.

"I get excited," she said, speaking carefully, "but it's not like the magazines."

She could not explain. Something separated her from Josephine, for the first time in her life. Josephine seemed to feel it, too. She sighed and pushed her pie away, lighting a cigarette and looking out at the rain. "Well," she said, "at least you're happy."

It was worse each time they saw each other. Josephine married, moved into a small ramshackle house only blocks from where she grew up, and had several robust children. She continued to paint in her free time, and Lucy's only recollection of her house, which she saw once, was a huge canvas hanging on one wall: a wild assemblage of red slashes and tumultuous grays. It reminded her of paintings she and Parker had seen in European museums.

Lucy remembers Josephine's soft hips and thighs, the warmth and strength of her hands. She must enjoy sex, Lucy thinks, for even as a child Josephine was passionate, romantic. She lacked Lucy's own self-consciousness, whatever it was that made her hide away the honeymoon bathing suits.

Lucy looks down the beach at the bungalow. She thinks of the couple sleeping inside, their tanned naked limbs sprawled under the twirling ceiling fan. A warm glow fills her, as though she, too, shared in their exhausted delight. The light has begun to deepen, coaxing the white sand to gold. Overhead, the palm trees make a sound like rainfall. The sun casts a pale ribbon of light across the trembling sea. Lucy looks around her tenderly, overcome by the sheer beauty of the scene. She will describe it in her letter to Josephine, for it is exactly the sort of thing Josephine will want to know.

That hour has arrived when sunbathers stretch and collect their belongings from the cooling sand. Lucy waits for Parker, who is moving down the beach. She is glad to see him.

"Happy?" Parker asks, for she is smiling. She holds out both hands for him to pull her from her chair, then kisses his ear. Parker smells of soap and aftershave. His hair is neatly combed, and he wears trousers with a loose Polynesian-style shirt. There is something jaunty in his air.

"I thought I'd go on up to the terrace and watch the sun set while you get ready," he says. "Why not let's try that fish place down the road for a change, since it's our last night."

"Perfect!" says Lucy. She collects her magazines and stuffs them in the bag. "How's the war coming?"

He shakes his head, grinning like a boy. "Super," he says.

Lucy takes a shower and rubs scented lotion over her body. She stares at the closet for a long time, trying to decide whether to wear a pantsuit or the bright Polynesian dress Parker bought her as a souvenir. She puts on the dress and looks in the mirror. Its colors are similar to those the blond woman was wearing when she arrived at the hotel. Before she can change her mind, Lucy grabs her purse and leaves the bungalow, holding her white sandals in one hand as she makes her way back across the sand to the terrace. Parker is leaning back in his chair. On the table sit two exotic-looking cocktails, filled with pineapple pieces and small umbrellas.

"Wow," Parker says when he sees Lucy in the Polynesian dress. She looks down, determined not to feel ashamed. Parker keeps glancing at her as he drinks. "That dress is something," he says.

After two cocktails they leave for the restaurant. It takes a long time to reach it, and normally Lucy would have wished they'd taken a taxi. But tonight she follows the twists and curves of road with a joyous sense of adventure. A smudge of fuchsia lingers just above the sea. Already a gravel of stars fills the sky. The moon, like the Tahitian sun, shines with abnormal vehemence.

The restaurant is a thatched hut filled with the smell of broiling fish. Flowers and vines dangle from the ceiling, and there is no floor, just cool white sand. Beside the grill lie heaps of gleaming sea creatures, blue-green parrot fish with gaping mouths, tangles of lobsters and crabs.

"Reminds me a little of that place in Kenya," Parker says when they reach their table, a block of wood wedged into the sand.

"Much better!" Lucy says, for the restaurant has a thrilling, exotic atmosphere. She will mention it in her letter to Josephine. She glances down and notices her Polynesian dress, which she has forgotten she is wearing. It looks perfect here.

Parker orders champagne. Lucy can see that he feels it, too, whatever she is feeling. There is a look he gets when he is excited, a puffy, breathless look, as if something inside him were swelling against his edges. His cheeks are flushed.

"Are you thinking about the war?" she asks.

He nods, and the flush spreads farther along his cheeks.

"Tell me about it," she says, really curious.

"I'm developing a position," he says. "An argument. My own as opposed to other people's. That's what history is, just a lot of arguments."

"And you've come up with your argument by reading theirs?"

"Yup. And disagreeing."

"I see. So what will you do with it? Your argument."

"I'll prove it," says Parker. "It'll take a lot of research."

"Will you have the time?"

Running the company takes long, steady hours of work. Parker rarely has free time, except on vacation.

"That's a question," he says, looking off toward the grill. "That's a question." He adds under his breath, "I miss it."

Lucy looks up. He has never said this before.

There is a pause. Parker glances down and flicks his wedding ring against the table. Lucy looks across the restaurant, not even surprised to discover the blond woman and her lover standing at the entrance. It is as if she were expecting them. The woman adjusts the purple flower in her hair. She, too, wears a Polynesian dress.

"Parker," Lucy says suddenly, "do you think it was right for you to give it up?"

She knows she has broken some tacit code in asking this. Parker is silent. He opens his mouth to speak, but doesn't. "I don't know," he finally says.

Lucy wants to press the point, but is afraid of pushing him too far. She waits, almost holding her breath, the way one does in the presence of a squirrel or a bird that will scramble away at the slightest jolt.

"I loved history," he says. "It was exciting."

As the maître d' leads the young couple to their table, the blond woman pauses at the grill and looks at the fish. Timidly she reaches out to press the shining scales of one.

"The funny part is," Parker says, "somehow I made a choice. I don't even know when. Only after it was made, I noticed that I just—"

"Thought differently?"

"Yes! That's right!" He seems elated that she understands. "That's what it was, I thought differently. But what bothers me . . ."

The man and woman sit down and hold hands. The blond hair falls in a curtain down the woman's back.

"What bothers me is . . . ." He can't seem to finish. One hand waves halfheartedly, trying to conjure the sentence.

"Money?" Lucy says very gently. "That somehow it was the money?"

Parker drops his hand. They look at one another in silence.

The meal is superb. Lucy and Parker linger at the restaurant a long time, long after the other couple has left. They drink a bottle of white wine and listen to the wind rattle the palm trees outside. It is as if they were afraid to go, as if, when they emerge from this den of white sand and rainbow-colored fish, a spell will break.

Finally they make their way back to the hotel. The moon has grown brittle and white overhead, and the warm wind scatters silver light across the sea. Lucy and Parker are drunk. They lean against each other for support, giggling like children as they make their way along the twisting road.

When they reach their bungalow, Lucy goes to the back deck and stands at the rail, watching the sea. She can hear Parker undressing inside, and finds that she is eager to make love tonight. The other bungalows are dark. Wind billows her dress, flooding it like a tent. Without looking away from the sea, Lucy unties the dress and lets the wind pull it from her. She stands naked, holding the dress at one corner, allowing the warm wind to engulf her.

The following year, Lucy and Parker visit Santa Barbara. They have flown there to meet with clients of Parker's, but will take several days to shop and enjoy the sun. After leaving their luggage at the hotel, they meander to a seafood restaurant at the tip of a long pier.

Lucy sits facing the ocean. Sunlight does a shrill dance on the water's surface, and she fumbles for her sunglasses. She can hardly see the waitress, who asks whether they would like drinks. When the woman returns with two iced teas, Lucy glances at her and jumps. It is the blond woman from Bora Bora.

Parker is poring over his menu, squinting through his reading glasses and holding it at a distance from his face.

"Did you see her?" Lucy hisses, plucking at his sleeve when the waitress has left.

"See who?"

"The waitress!"

Parker stares at his wife.

"Don't you remember? I'm sure it's the same person!"

"Same person as who?"

"On Bora Bora! That blond woman we saw."

"Are you serious? That was ages ago."

Lucy leans back in frustrated silence. But she is excited, and she twists around in her chair to catch another glimpse of the waitress. The woman returns to the table with her order pad, and Lucy looks directly into her face. There is no doubt that it is the same woman—the blond hair, the long, perfect limbs.

"Can I take your order?" she asks.

It occurs to Lucy that she has never heard the woman speak.

"Crab salad," says Parker.

There is a silence. Both the waitress and Parker look at Lucy, waiting. "For you, ma'am?" the waitress asks.

"Oh, I'll have . . ." Lucy fumbles, looking down at the menu. "The same. Crab salad."

Lucy sits, watching the sea. She tries to remember Bora Bora. Like all their vacations, that one has faded, blurred with other hotels, other beaches.

"Parker?"

"Mmm?" He is going over some numbers the Santa Barbara clients have given him.

"What ever happened with the Crimean War?"

He looks at her in confusion.

"On Bora Bora. You were so excited . . . you wanted to do research, remember?"

"Vaguely."

She can tell he does not want to be interrupted, but persists. "What ever happened to that idea?"

Parker shrugs, frowning. "No time," he says. "Got to make a living."

The waitress returns with the salads. Lucy watches her pour dressing over them and tries to recall the woman she watched on the beach a year before. But already the vision has begun to cloud. No, Lucy thinks, looking down at her plate, no, this cannot be the same woman after all.

When the waitress has gone, Lucy looks at Parker. He is drumming his fingers on the quilted place mat, staring at the bay. Lucy hears his stomach murmur. She watches this man who is her husband, his brown arms with their sparse coating of hair, his pale, timid eyes. She feels an urge to say something to him, but can think of nothing worthwhile: A comment on the view? The menu? The night ahead? Their conversation is exhausted.

Instead, she thinks of Josephine. It has been a long time since Lucy recalled her old friend, but suddenly, now, she can see her exactly. Lucy pictures Josephine seated in Parker's chair, leaning forward, resting her chin on one hand. She is poised to listen.

"Wait, wait, back up," Lucy hears her command. "So you're having lunch on a pier—describe it to me. Is the sun out?"

It's low, Lucy thinks, it drifts on the water in flakes. There are gulls with gray-tipped wings and a dot of red on their beaks. The ocean shakes like reams of fluttering silk.

Josephine laughs. It is a cackle of wonderment, a whistle of envy and delight.

"I see it," she says. "I see it exactly."

And for a moment the world ignites, it blazes around them with exquisite radiance. Each detail is right.

"Look where you are," Josephine says. "Look! You're in the perfect spot."

For a magnificent instant, Lucy believes it.

SISTERS
OF THE MOON

Silas has a broken head. It happened sometime last night, outside
The Limited on Geary and Powell. None of us saw. Silas says the
fight was over a woman, and that he won it. "But you look like all
bloody shit, my friend," Irish says, laughing, rolling the words off
his accent. Silas says we should've seen the other guy.

He adjusts the bandage on his head and looks up at the palm
trees, which make a sound over Union Square like it's raining. Silas
has that strong kind of shape, like high school guys who you know
could pick you up and carry you like a bag. But his face is old. He
wears a worn-out army jacket, the pockets always fat with something. Once, he pulled out a silver thimble and pushed it into my
hand, not saying one word. It can't be real silver, but I've kept it.

I think Silas fought in Vietnam. Once he said, "It's 1974, and I'm still alive," like he couldn't believe it.

"So where is he?" Irish asks, full of humor. "Where is this bloke with half his face gone?"

Angel and Liz start laughing, I don't know why. "Where's this woman you fought for?" is what I want to ask.

Silas shrugs, grinning. "Scared him away."

San Francisco is ours, we've signed our name on it a hundred times: SISTERS OF THE MOON. On the shiny tiles inside the Stockton Tunnel, across those buildings like blocks of salt on the empty piers near the Embarcadero. Silver plus another color, usually blue or red. Angel and Liz do the actual painting. I'm the lookout. While they're spraying the paint cans, I get scared to death. To calm down, I'll say to myself, If the cops come, or if someone stops his car to yell at us, I'll just walk away from Angel and Liz, like I never saw them before in my life. Afterward, when the paint is wet and we bounce away on the balls of our feet, I get so ashamed, thinking, What if they knew? They'd probably ditch me, which would be worse than getting caught—even going to jail. I'd be all alone in the universe.

Most people walk through Union Square on their way someplace else. Secretaries, businessmen. The Park, we call it. But Silas and Irish and the rest are always here. They drift out, then come back. Union Square is their own private estate.

Watching over the square like God is the St. Francis Hotel, with five glass elevators sliding up and down its polished face. Stoned, Angel and Liz and I spend hours sitting on benches with our heads back, waiting for the elevators to all line up on top. Down, up, down—even at 5 A.M. they're moving. The St. Francis never sleeps.

Angel and Liz expect to be famous, and I believe it. Angel just turned fifteen. I'm only five months younger, and Liz is younger than me. But I'm the baby of us. Smoking pot in Union Square, I still worry who will see.

We've been talking for a week about dropping acid. I keep stalling. Today we go ahead and buy it, from a boy with a runny nose and dark, anxious eyes. Across the street is I. Magnin, and I get a sick feeling that my stepmother is going to come out the revolving doors with packages under her arms. She's a buyer for the shoe department at Saks, and in the afternoon she likes to walk around and view the competition.

Angel leans against a palm tree, asking in her Southern voice if the acid is pure and how much we should take to get off and how long the high will last us. She's got her shirt tied up so her lean stomach shows. Angel came from Louisiana a year ago with her mother's jazz band. I adore her. She goes wherever she wants, and the world just forms itself around her.

"What are you looking at?" Liz asks me. She's got short, curly black hair and narrow blue eyes.

"Nothing."

"Yes, you are," she says. "All the time. Just watching everything."

"So?"

"So, when are you going to do something?" She says it like she's joking.

I get a twisting in my stomach. "I don't know," I say. I glance at Angel, but she's talking to the dealer. At least she didn't hear us.

Liz and I look at I. Magnin. Her mother could walk out of there as easily as mine, but Liz doesn't care. I get the feeling she's waiting for something like that to happen, a chance to show Angel how far she can go.

We find Irish begging on Powell Street. "Can you spare any part of a million dollars?" he asks the world, spreading his arms wide. Irish has a big blond face and wavy hair and eyes that are almost purple—I mean it. One time, he says, he got a thousand-dollar bill—an Arab guy just handed it over. That was before we knew Irish.

"My lassies," he calls out, and we get the hug of those big arms, all three of us. He inhales from Angel's hair, which is dark brown and flips into wings on both sides of her face. She's still a virgin. In Angel this seems beautiful, like a precious glass bowl you can't believe didn't break yet. One time, in Union Square, this Australian guy took hold of her hair and pulled it back, back, so the tendons of her throat showed through the skin, and Angel was laughing at first and so was the guy, but then he leaned down and kissed her mouth and Irish knocked him away, shouting, "Hey, motherfucker, can't you see she's still a child?"

"What nice presents have you brought?" Irish asks now.

Angel opens the bag to show the acid. I check around for cops and catch Liz watching me, a look on her face like she wants to laugh.

"When shall we partake?" Irish asks, reaching out with his cap to a lady in a green raincoat, who shakes her head like he should know better, then drops in a quarter. Irish could have any kind of life, I think—he just picked this one.

"Not yet," Angel says. "Too light."

"Tonight," Liz says, knowing I won't be there.

Angel frowns. "What about Tally?"

I look down, startled and pleased to be remembered.

"Tomorrow?" Angel asks me.

I can't help pausing for a second, holding this feeling of everyone waiting for my answer. Then someone singing "Gimme Shelter"
distracts them. I wish I'd just said it.

"Tomorrow's fine."

The singer turns out to be a guy named Fleece, who I don't know. I
mean, I've seen him, he's part of the gang of Irish and Silas and them
who hang out in the Park. Angel says these guys are in their thirties,
but they look older than that and act younger, at least around us.
There are women, too, with red eyes and heavy makeup, and mostly
they act loud and happy, but when they get dressed up, there are
usually holes in their stockings, or at least a run. They don't like us
—Angel especially.

Angel hands me the acid bag to hold while she lights up a joint.
Across the Park I see three cops walking—I can almost hear the
squeak of their boots. I cover the bag with my hand. I see Silas on
another bench. His bandage is already dirty.

"Tally's scared," Liz says. She's watching me, that expression
in her eyes like the laughter behind them is about to come pushing
out.

The others look at me, and my heart races. "I'm not."

In Angel's eyes I see a flash of cold. Scared people make her
moody, like they remind her of something she wants to forget.
"Scared of what?" she says.

"I'm not."

Across the square, Silas adjusts the bandage over his eyes.
Where is this woman he fought for? I wonder. Why isn't she with
him now?

"I don't know," Liz says. "What're you scared of, Tally?"

I look right at Liz. There's a glittery challenge in her eyes but also something else, like she's scared, too. She hates me, I think. We're friends, but she hates me.

Irish tokes from the joint in the loudest way, like it's a tube connecting him to the last bit of oxygen on earth. When he exhales, his face gets white. "What's she scared of?" he says, and laughs faintly. "The world's a bloody terrifying place."

At home that night I can't eat. I'm too thin, like a little girl, even though I'm fourteen. Angel loves to eat, and I know that's how you get a figure, but my body feels too small. It can't hold anything extra.

"How was school?" my stepmother asks.

"Fine."

"Where have you been since then?"

"With Angel and those guys. Hanging around." No one seems to notice my Southern accent.

My father looks up. "Hanging around doing what?"

"Homework."

"They're in biology together," my stepmother explains.

Across the table the twins begin to whimper. As he leans over their baby heads, my father's face goes soft—I see it even through his beard. The twins are three years old, with bright red hair. Tomorrow I'll tie up my shirt, I think, like Angel did. So what if my stomach is white?

"I'm spending the night tomorrow," I say. "At Angel's."

He wipes applesauce from the babies' mouths. I can't tell if he means to refuse or is just distracted. "Tomorrow's Saturday," I tell him, just in case.

We spend all day at Angel's, preparing. Her mom went to Mexico with the band she plays violin for, and won't be back for a month. Candles, powdered incense from the Mystic Eye, on Broadway, a paint set, sheets of creamy paper, Pink Floyd records stacked by the stereo, and David Bowie, and Todd Rundgren, and "Help Me," of course—Joni Mitchell's new hit, which we worship.

Angel lives six blocks from Union Square in a big apartment south of Market Street, with barely any walls. A foil pyramid hangs from the ceiling over her bed. All day we keep checking the square for Irish, but he's disappeared.

At sundown we go ahead without him. Candles on the window-sills, the white rug vacuumed. We cut the pills with a knife, and each of us takes one-third of all three so we're sure to get the same dose. I'm terrified. It seems wrong that such a tiny thing could do so much. But I feel Liz watching me, waiting for one wrong move, and I swallow in silence.

Then we wait. Angel does yoga, arching her back, pressing her palms to the floor with her arms bent. I've never seen anyone so limber. The hair rushes from her head in a flood of black, like it could stain the rug. Liz's eyes don't move from her.

When the acid starts to work, we all lie together on her mother's huge four-poster bed, Angel in the middle. She holds one of our hands in each of hers. Angel has the kind of skin that tans in a minute, and beautiful, snaking veins. I feel the blood moving in her. We wave our hands above our faces and watch them leave trails. I feel Angel warm beside me and think how I'll never love anyone this much, how without her I would disappear.

The city at night is full of lights and water and hills like piles of sand. We struggle to climb them. Empty cable cars totter past. The sky is a sheet of black paper with tiny holes poked in it. The Chinatown sidewalks smell like salt and flesh. It's 3 A.M. Planes drift overhead like strange fish.

Market Street, a steamy puddle at every curb. We find our way down alleys, our crazy eyes making diamonds of the shattered glass that covers the streets and sidewalks. Nothing touches us. We float under the orange streetlamps. My father, the twins—everything but Angel and Liz and me just fades into nothing, the way the night used to disappear when my real mother tucked me into bed, years ago.

In the Broadway Tunnel I grab for the spray cans. "Let me," I cry, breathless. Angel and Liz are too stoned to care. We have green and silver. I hold one can in each fist, shake them up, and spray huge round letters, like jaws ready to swallow me. I breathe in the paint fumes and they taste like honey. Tiny dots of cool paint fall on my face and eyelashes and stay there. Traffic ricochets past, but I don't care tonight—I don't care. In the middle of painting I turn to Angel and Liz and cry, "This is it, this is it!" and they nod excitedly, like they already knew, and then I start to cry. We hug in the Broadway Tunnel. "This is it," I sob, clinging to Angel and Liz, their warm shoulders. I hear them crying, too, and think, It will be like this always. From now on, nothing can divide us.

It seems like hours before I notice the paint cans still in my hands and finish the job. SISTERS OF THE MOON.

It blazes.

We make our way to Union Square. Lo and behold, there is Irish, holding court with a couple of winos and a girl named Pamela, who I've heard is a prostitute. Irish looks different tonight—he's got big, swashbuckling sleeves that flap like sails in the wind. He's grand. As we walk toward him, blinking in the liquidy light, an amazement at his greatness overwhelms us. He is a great man, Irish. We're lucky to know him.

Irish scoops Angel into his arms. "My beloved," he says. "I've been waiting all night for you." And he kisses her full on the lips—a deep, long kiss that Angel seems at first to resist. Then she relaxes, like always. I feel a small, sharp pain, like a splinter of glass in my heart. But I'm not surprised. It was always going to happen, I think. We were always waiting.

Angel and Irish draw apart and look at each other. Liz hovers near them. Pamela gets up and walks away, into the shadows. I sit on the bench with the winos and stare up at the St. Francis Hotel.

"You're high," Irish says to Angel. "So very high."

"What about you? Your pupils are gone," she says.

Irish laughs. He laughs and laughs, opening up his mouth like the world could fit in it. Irish might live on the streets, but his teeth are white. "I'll see you in Heaven," he says.

On the St. Francis Hotel the glass elevators float. Two reach the top, and two more rise slowly to join them. They hang there, all four, and I hold my breath as the fifth approaches and will the others not to move until it gets there. I keep perfectly still, pushing the last one up with my eyes until it reaches the top, and there they are, in a perfect line, all five.

I turn to show Angel and Liz, but they're gone. I see them walking away with Irish, Angel in the middle, Liz clutching at her arm like the night could pull them apart. It's Liz who looks back at me. Our eyes meet, and I feel like she's talking out loud, I understand so perfectly. If I move fast, now, I can keep her from winning. But the thought makes me tired. I don't move. Liz turns away. I think I see a bouncing in her steps, but I stay where I am.

They turn to ghosts in the darkness and vanish. My teeth start to chatter. It's over. Angel is gone, I think, and I start to cry. She just walked away.

Then I hear a rushing noise. It's a sound like time passing, years racing past, so all of a sudden I'm much older, a grown-up woman looking back to when she was a girl in Union Square. And I realize that even if Angel never thinks of me again, at some point I'll get up and take the bus home.

The winos have drifted off. By my Mickey Mouse watch it's 5 A.M. I notice someone crossing the square—it's Silas, the dirty bandage still around his head. I yell out to him.

He comes over slowly, like it hurts to walk. He sits down next to me. For a long time we just sit, not talking. Finally I ask, "Was it really over a woman?"

Silas shakes his head. "Just a fight," he says. "Just another stupid fight."

I straighten my legs so that my sneakers meet in front of me. They're smudged but still white. "I'm hungry," I say.

"Me, too," Silas says. "But everything's closed." Then he says, "I'm leaving town."

"To where?"

"South Carolina. My brother's store. Called him up today."

"How come?"

"Had enough," he says. "Just finally had enough."

I know there's something I should say, but I don't know what. "Is he nice," I ask, "your brother?"

Silas grins. I see the young part of him then, the kind of mischief boys have. "He's the meanest bastard I know."

"What about Irish?" I ask. "Won't you miss Irish and those guys?"

"Irish is a dead man."

I stare at Silas.

"Believe it," he says. "In twenty years no one will remember him."

Twenty years. In twenty years I'd be thirty-four years old, my stepmother's age. It would be 1994. And suddenly I think, Silas is right—Irish is dead. And Angel, too, and maybe even Liz. Right now is their perfect, only time. It will sweep them away. But Silas was always outside it.

I put my hand in my pocket and find the thimble. I pull it out. "You gave me this," I tell him.

Silas looks at the thimble like he's never seen it. Then he says, "That's real silver."

Maybe he wants it back to sell, for his trip to South Carolina. I leave the thimble in my hand so that if Silas wants it he can just take it. But he doesn't. We both look at the thimble. "Thanks," I say.

We lean back on the bench. My high is wearing off. I have a feeling in my chest like feathers, like a bird waking up and brushing against my ribs. The elevators rise and fall, like signals.

"Always watching," Silas says, looking at me. "Those big eyes, always moving."

I nod, ashamed. "But I never do anything," I say. And all of a sudden I know, I know why Angel left me.

Silas frowns. "Sure you do. You watch," he says, "which is what'll save you."

I shrug. But the longer we sit, the more I realize he's right— what I do is watch. I'm like Silas, I think. In twenty years I'll still be alive.

On one side the sky is getting light, like a lid is being lifted up. I watch it, trying to see the day coming, but I can't. All of a sudden the sky is just bright.

"I wonder what people will look like in 1994," I say.

Silas considers. "Twenty years? Probably look like us again."

"Like you and me?" I'm disappointed.

"Oh yeah," Silas says with a wry grin. "Wishing they'd been here the first time."

I look at the blue bandanna tied around his wrist, his torn-up jeans and army jacket with a Grateful Dead skull on one pocket. When I'm thirty-four, tonight will be a million years ago, I think— the St. Francis Hotel and the rainy palm tree sounds, Silas with the bandage on his head—and this makes me see how everything now is precious, how someday I'll know I was lucky to be here.

"I'll remember Irish," I say loudly. "I'll remember everyone. In twenty years."

Silas looks at me curiously. Then he touches my face, tracing my left cheekbone almost to my ear. His finger is warm and rough, and I have the thought that to Silas my skin must feel soft. He studies the paint on the tip of his finger, and smiles. He shows me. "Silver," he says.